20 MILLION MILES TO EARTH

SCIENCE FICTION NOVEL

ANC

20 MILLION MILES TO EARTH

35¢

BY HENRY SLESAR—

Based on

Columbia Pictures'

Shock-Thriller

This Outerspace Monster Leveled Cities — Ravaged Earth

Courtesy Randall D. Larson

20 MILLION MILES TO EARTH

By
Henry Slesar

20 Million Miles to Earth: From Movie to Novel
By Randall D. Larson

Philip J. Riley's

NIGHTMARE SERIES

BearManor Media

BearManor Media
P.O. Box 1129
Duncan, OK 73534-1129

Phone: 580-252-3547
Fax: 814-690-1559

www.bearmanormedia.com

20 Million Miles to Earth by Henry Slesar
First published by Amazing Stories (Ziff-Davis Publishing)-1957
First Bearmanor Media edition 2013

Edited and designed by Philip J. Riley ©2013

A copy of the original *Amazing Stories* novelette courtesy of Randall D Larson.

The Nightmares Series is being published to preserve original movie tie-in novels that were printed many years ago, on the old style pulp paper. It will also include several very rare movie tie-in titles in the horror film genre. We hope these reprints will allow them to last into the new century.

OTHER BOOKS IN THE
NIGHTMARE SERIES

Brides of Dracula by Dean Owen
The Revenge of Frankenstein
The Raven by Eunice Sudak
The Bride of Frankenstein by Michael Egremont
Dr. Cyclops - By Will Garth & Henry Kuttner
The Pit and the Pendulum by Lee Sheridan

20 Million Miles to Earth: From Movie to Novel
By Randall D. Larson

"Great scientific advances are oftentimes sudden accomplished facts before most of us are even dimly aware of them. Breathtakingly unexpected, for example, was the searing flash that announced the atomic age. Equally unexpected was the next gigantic stride whcn Man moved out of his very orbit to a point more than 20 million miles to Earth."
- Opening narration

Released in 1957, "20 Million Miles to Earth" is a superior giant-monster-runs-amok movie in a decade that was swarming with multiple species of them. Written by Bob Williams and Christopher Knopf (from an original story by Ray Harryhausen), the film has an engaging storyline about an American spaceship returning from an expedition to Venus that crash lands upon its return to Earth, unleashing its captured specimen: a diminutive lizard-like creature that begins to grow to giant proportions once exposed to Earth's atmosphere. The film was Harryhausen's third in partnership with producer Charles M. Schneer, the productive collaboration that brought forth all of Harryhausen's work from "It Came From Beneath the Sea" in 1955 through 1981's "Clash of the Titans." Unlike other giant-monster-on-the-loose movies of the decade such as "The Giant Behemoth," "The Black Scorpion," and Harryhausen's own "The Beast from 20,000 Fathoms" and "It Came From Beneath the Sea," "20 Million Miles to Earth" made an attempt to create a sympathetic monster whose acts of violence are the result of self-defense and mistreatment by the human population.

"This was Harryhausen's 'King Kong'," wrote Bill Warren in *Watching The Skies*, noting that, like the giant ape of that 1933 classic

7

film, it's about "an essentially innocent monster [that] is brought to civilization, where it runs amok and then is killed.[1] Emboldened by remarkably fluid animation and attention to detail, Harryhausen's stop-motion animation of "20 Million Miles to Earth" also benefitted from very effective lighting set-ups that allowed the animated models to fit convincingly into the live action background, and the effective mixture of story and special effects has made many regard "20 Million Miles to Earth" as Harryhausen's best black-and-white feature film.

Making "20 Million Miles to Earth"

The success of their first two films ("It Came From Beneath the Sea" and 1956's "Earth vs. the Flying Saucers") prompted Schneer to form his own production company, named Morningside Prods (named for the street, Morningside Drive, where Schneer lived while attending Columbia College in New York). An arrangement was made with Columbia Pictures for a 12-picture financing and distribution deal, which also allowed Morningside to use studio facilities for filming and post-production. "20 Million Miles to Earth" would be Morningside's first production, and also Harryhausen's first film to emerge from one of his own ideas.

Writing in *An Animated Life*, Harryhausen explained that he got the idea for "20 Million Miles to Earth" back in 1954 when he wrote a story outline called "The Cyclops," which described a spaceship crash landing into Lake Michigan, resulting in the release of a sizeable, one-eyed creature that Chicago.[2] Many story elements – its escape from captivity, its fight with an elephant, and its rampage through a city – were retained into the film's shooting script. Harryhausen put his Cyclops creature on hold until "The 7th Voyage of Sinbad" in 1958 and instead changed the creature into a two-legged reptilian, mustachioed beast with three clawed hands, a long forked tail, and a bellowing roar that he called Ymir (partially inspired by the snow god of Norse mythology[3]). "I decided on a basic humanoid form because I wanted audiences to sympathize with it, and you can't do that if it's totally alien," Harryhausen wrote in. "But to ensure that audiences knew it was alien, I added a hint of dinosaur and slowly the Ymir evolved."[4]

Elsewhere, Harryhausen described the many changes the creature went through from its metamorphosis from Cyclops to Ymir: "I didn't want him too grotesque, because I'd lose my audience. So I gave him a human torso and a sort of dinosaur tail, with the legs of a satyr. The head and face was a cross between a number of fish that I looked at."[5]

The film's working title was "The Giant Ymir," and thus the creature became known by that designation even when the title was changed to "20 Million Miles to Earth." The creature is never actually referred to by name in the released film (reportedly there was concern that international audiences might confuse the term "Ymir" with the customary Arabic potentate title, "Emir").

Harryhausen continued to develop the story with writing associate Charlotte Knight[6] (she was also an actress, mostly for television), who collaborated with him on several of the "Mother Goose Stories" shorts he made in the earlier 1950s. With titles and locations changing, Harryhausen and Knight finally settled on Rome (partly because of Harryhausen's desire to vacation there during shooting). "Rome was a romantic spot and I rather fancied having the Ymir in the final reel leave a mass of new ruins among the old," Harryhausen wrote in his *Film Fantasy Scrapbook*. "At that period of film-making it was important to include the ultimate in mass devastation, if one even hoped to sell an idea."[7]

While Knight reworked the storyline, Harryhausen began to draw, producing a number of detailed sketches to be included in his presentation of the proposed project to the studio. These drawings would also be vital to the later screenwriters when they created the actual shooting script, as Harryhausen explained: "Our script is not built completely by the writer because the visuals are so important in our type of film. We had to start with the visuals because that's what we're concentrating on, to get the biggest impression. The writer's main job was to tie all these visuals together into a coherent story…"[8]

In the case of "20 Million Miles to Earth," screenwriters Williams and Knopf enmeshed those visuals into a credible, if somewhat simple and formulaic, monster-on-the-loose storyline, but one with fairly nice character development and dramatic excitement that flowed naturally out of the unfolding story. Robert Creighton (Bob) Williams was a veteran of B-movie scripts, having written dozens of Westerns for Republic Pictures in the 1940s. His co-screenwriter on "20 Million Miles to Earth," Christopher Knopf, was just starting out in the 1950s; this was his second scripting job and he would go on to write extensively for episodic television through the early 1990s.

The film was directed by Nathan Juran, who'd been an Oscar-winning art director before moving into directing in 1952 with the Boris Karloff thriller, "The Black Castle." His history in art direction made him an ideal choice to work with Harryhausen because the two craftsmen were able to understand each other's needs. Juran proved to be an efficient director who kept within both budget and shooting schedule; he would go on to direct Harryhausen's "7th Voyage of Sinbad" (1958) and "The First Men In The Moon" (1964), as well as such genre favorites as "The Deadly Mantis" (1957), "Attack of the 50 Foot Woman" (1958, as "Nathan Hertz") and the Sinbad-like "Jack The Giant Killer" (1962).

For the cast, Schneer and Harryhausen brought aboard a group of competent actors experienced in B-movies, many of whom they'd worked with before. William Hopper played main hero Col. Calder, sole survivor of the rocket ship crash, as a self-confident military leader with a carefully hidden heart. Hopper had been a bit player since the 1930s, with uncredited roles in more than a hundred B-movies, graduating to larger parts in the 1950s. He played the spaceship's doctor in George Pal's "Conquest of Space" (1955), played the father of the wicked girl in "The Bad Seed" (1956), and co-starred as the consulting paleontologist in Juran's "The Deadly

Mantis" (1957). Hopper is now best remembered for playing private detective Paul Drake on TV's "Perry Mason" (1957-66). As Hopper's love interest, medical student Marisa, Joan Taylor was cast. She played in B-movies throughout the 1950s, including the Roger Corman Western "Apache Woman" (1955) and had been the female lead in "Earth vs. the Flying Saucers." The year after appearing in "20 Million Miles to Earth," Taylor transitioned to television, guest starring on many shows and having a regular role on "The Riflemen" (1960-62 seasons). John Zaremba, a recognizable supporting player in more than 150 movies and television since 1950, played the film's voice of science, Dr. Uhl. He'd played a Power Company Chief in "The Magnetic Monster" (1953), been a professor in "Earth vs. the Flying Saucers," would be a police lieutenant in "Frankenstein's Daughter" (1958) and, moving to television in 1959, became a one of the scientists responsible for Irwin Allen's "The Time Tunnel" (1966-67). Another familiar face from 1950s B-movies, Thomas Henry, was cast as Major General McIntosh, Calder's commander; he'd been acting since the late 1940s with dozens of character roles, usually as a gruff senior officer, and had played a similar role in "Earth vs. the Flying Saucers" and Bert I. Gordon's "Beginning of the End" (1957). He later played in Herman Cohen's "Blood of Dracula" (1957) and "How To Make A Monster" (1958), and had dozens of TV appearances throughout the '60s, including three episodes of "Perry Mason" with Hopper. Child star Bart Braverman played the crafty Sicilian boy Pepe, who discovers the Ymir's gelatinous egg. Braverman began acting at the age of 5 in 1955; as an adult he's been a frequent guest star on television, best known as Binzer on "Vega$" (1978-81).

Of the cast, only William Hopper appeared in the scenes actually filmed in Rome (most of those being his direction of the soldiers at the Colosseum as they face off against the Ymir). Harryhausen had spent two weeks in mid-1956 scouting locations and determined, then returned that Fall with Hopper and a small crew to film the necessary background shots he would need for his animated sequences. Italian extras were used to stand in for his secondary cast in the long shots (and these would mix nicely when edited with shots of the real cast filmed in Los Angeles). Numerous scenes were filmed at historical sites as the Roman Forum, Temple of Saturn, Colosseum, as well as the Tiber River and various city streets; the Borghese Gallery exterior and the arches of Hadrian's Viaduct would serve as background imagery for the fight between Ymir and the elephant. All of these would give the modest film a sufficient aura of grandeur into which Harryhausen could insert his animated Ymir. Italian extras stood in for the secondary cast in long shots, with close attention to costuming and general appearance. Lawrence W. Butler (an Oscar winner for visual effects in Alexander Korda's 1940 "Thief of Bagdad" who had also worked on "Casablanca") served as very competent 2nd Unit Director, aided by Italian assistant director Octavio Oppo (later Sergio Leone's production manager on "For A Few Dollars More"), working with an Italian crew to film establishing shots and crowd reactions on location. The Italian government supplied tanks and other military vehicles and soldiers to engage the Ymir at the Colosseum; Mike Hanken, writing in *Ray Harryhausen: Master of Majicks (Vol. 2)*, notes that the production wound up paying to replace the tarmac in the streets around the Colosseum that had been badly torn up by the tank treads during the filming![9]

When the Italian sequences were completed, Juran came on-board to begin filming the live action scenes with the primary cast in Los Angeles. Locations such as the Corriganville Ranch (the Ymir's capture by the helicopter), the former Edison Electrical Plant in El Segundo (the interior of the rocket ship), and the Columbia Pictures back lot (Dr. Leonardo's trailer home, the laboratory of the Rome Zoo, etc.).

While Juran was at work, Harryhausen was busy with the meticulous, single-handed animation process taking place in his small studio. Using miniature three-dimensional models molded over articulating metal armatures, Harryhausen animated the models one frame at a time (24 frames per second of running time), keeping track of each element involved in the scene – creature, other animals, collapsing miniature structures, matted foreground images and rear-projected background images – every step of the way. The process had been developed by Harryhausen's mentor, Willis O'Brien in films like "The Lost World" (1925) and "King Kong" (1933); Harryhausen had worked with O'Brien on "Mighty Joe Young" (1949) and, for three decades since, made the process his own, eventually calling it "Dynamation" beginning with "7th Voyage of Sinbad." When "20 Million Miles to Earth" was released, somebody in Columbia's publicity department, learning about the term from "Sinbad's" pre-production planning, made up the term "Electrolitic Dynamation" to describe "@0 Million's" visual effects technology in "20 Million Miles" publicity pressbook and radio spots. No such actual process existed.

"20 Million Miles to Earth" allowed Harryhausen to realize some of finest animated effects to date. 1953's "The Beast From 20,000 Fathoms," had featured a prehistoric rhedosaurus, awakened by a nuclear bomb test, marvelously brought to life by Harryhausen's meticulous stop-motion animation technique. But the Ymir of "20 Million Miles to Earth" showed great enhancements in Harryhausen's art after just four years, including experiences learned on 1955's "It Came From Beneath the Sea" and 1956's "Earth vs. The Flying Saucers." The Venusian beast interacted even more seamlessly with its environment using the technique he would later term "Dynamation," in which the model is animated between a rear-screen projected image and a foreground matte image, thus completing the illusion that the model exists within the live setting. For the first time, Harryhausen featured his main monster (like Kong's struggles against the Tyrannosaurus, Plesiosaurus, and Pteranodon) in ferocious battle with another animated creature, an angry elephant.

"The story has parallels to 'King Kong,' but it was written as a tribute, not as a pale copy, and reflecting my feelings about man's inhumanity to animals," Harryhausen wrote in *An Animated Life*. "This sentiment was evident in the final words of the outline: 'Nature clouds well its secrets. What have we to offer other planets, our fears, our hatreds, our destruction?' This sentiment was to survive into the final film but with a different approach."[10]

Because the production had been short of extras when it filmed the Italian scenes, Harryhausen stepped in to make a rare screen appearance in the movie – first as a man feeding peanuts to an elephant in the Rome zoo, and later as a member of the crowd fleeing from the same zoo when the Ymir has broken free.

Beyond its giant-monster-on-the-rampage scenario, "20 Million Miles to Earth" was especially interesting because the monster grew from doll size to gigantic proportions, allowing for some effective suspense scenes prior to emerging as a giant monster thriller. A very fine scene occurs early in the film when the man-sized Ymir gets loose in a barn, generating some fine moody suspense in the structure's deep shadows.

Along with the bellowing roars of the beast, the film's musical score gave voice to the film's dramatic elements and intensified its excitement. Unlike the close-knit collaboration Harryhausen would develop with composer Bernard Herrmann beginning with his next film, Columbia Pictures' Music Director Mischa Bakaleinikoff was assigned to generate a score for "20 Million Miles to Earth," which he did so through a patchwork of recycled music taken from the studio's music library, enhanced by original musical cues he composed himself. This was a common practice for B-movies throughout the '40 sand '50s. While much of the recycled library music is fairly generic, a lot of it fits and supports the movie well. "Bakaleinikoff realized that nothing in Columbia's music library was appropriate to underscore the Ymir, so he created a musical theme for the beast, as well as cues heard during the creature's initial appearances," explained '50s monster movie music expert David Schecter, who produced a CD that included the "20 Million Miles to Earth" score. "Of "2MMTE's" 95 cues, Bakaleinokoff wrote 49 of them, with a few being composed for prior pictures and others being multiple uses of the same cues."[11]

Of his brand new cues, Bakaleinikoff's four-note "creature" theme is most effective. Heard throughout the film, it becomes a ferocious ostinato accompanying the Ymir's escape from captivity and attack upon the Roman landscape. Introduced on a novachord (an early electronic keyboard) when Pepe finds the egg, Bakaleinikoff adds more instruments to the theme as the creature grows (woodwinds added during Ymir's birth, eventually performed with brass and then the full orchestra by the time of Ymir's showdown atop the Colosseum). As for the library tracks, they weren't simply edited into the film's soundtrack from library tapes; Bakaleinikoff re-orchestrated and re-recorded them to fit the particulars of this film. The recycled cues (bits and pieces from more than a dozen composers, originally written for previous Columbia films) include Miklós Rózsa's dramatic "Tambul's Death" from 1943's "Sahara" (when the helicopter drops the electric net over the Ymir), Daniele Amfitheatrof's "Trial and Escape" music from 1942's "Talk of the Town" (scenes of the Ymir feeding on sulfur), Max Steiner's "Evil Deed" from the 1955 western, "The Violent Men" (final moments of the Ymir/elephant fight), and others. A very short resolution from George Duning's music from the 1949 Western "Lust For Gold" (1949) concludes "20 Million Miles to Earth" with a warm spirit of accomplishment and relief as Calder and Marissa walk off, arm-in-arm.

Like Kong's famous confrontation atop New York City's Empire State Building, the Ymir's final face-off against the military occurs on the top of Rome's famous Colosseum, where he meets his end against the superior firepower of, to him, an alien enemy. "The Colosseum seemed a fitting end for our friend the Ymir," Harryhausen wrote in *Film Fantasy Scrapbook*. "The structure's height and circular design lent itself to some interesting compositions... Dramaturgy demand[ed] that the 'villain' should die in the most dramatic way possible. The top of the Colosseum offered this opportunity. Another 'must,' in my opinion, is that the 'villain' should die with a touch of pathos."[12]

"The inspired closing scenes, with the Ymir standing high upon the rim of the Colosseum, are images that stay in the mind forever," wrote Mike Hanken. "Ray's astonishing ability to emote through his models is never better displayed than here, giving the doomed creature undeniable pathos and bringing the audience fully on the side of the dying invader."[13] To underline that pathos and leave audiences with a note of reflective consideration, it was decided that the ending needed a tagline. Recalling the sentiment with which he'd closed his original outline, Harryhausen had the concluding line hastily written at the last minute, and spoken by Dr. Uhl: "Why is it always, always so costly for Man to move from the present to the future?" Harryhausen felt it worked rather well, if not as good as "King Kong's" closing line: "It wasn't the airplanes. It was beauty killed the beast." Writing in *An Animated Life*, Harryhausen stated: "The whole film was a message about man's fear and exploitation of the unknown, and that humans had assumed the Ymir was aggressive. After all, he only wanted to go home."[14]

The film would be Harryhausen and Schneer's last in black-and-white. While Harryhausen hoped to shoot "20 Million Miles to Earth" in color, its budget wasn't sufficient to do so, and 1958's "The 7th Voyage of Sinbad" would be his first to be shot in color (a 2007 home video release featured an expertly colorized rendition of "20 Million Miles to Earth," produced with Harryhausen's close participation). "20 Million Miles to Earth" would also, except for 1969's "The Valley of Gwangi," be Harryhausen's last monster-on-the-loose movie; the colorful fantasies that would follow would be drawn from Arabian and Greek mythology, and prehistoric life.

Novelizing "20 Million Miles to Earth" – Henry Slesar Meets the Ymir

Motion picture novelizations have existed almost as long as movies have. The "Photoplay Editions" were popular hardback books mostly published by Grosset & Dunlap in the USA during the 1920s and 30s; they mostly consisted of movie tie-in reprints of popular novels with cover images and photographs from the movies – books like A. Conan Doyle's *The Lost World*, Victor Hugo's *The Hunchback of Notre Dame* and Gaston Leroux's *The Phantom of the*

Opera were newly published to tie-in with their movie adaptations of the 1920s. In the 1930s it was Bram Stoker's *Dracula*, Mary Shelley's *Frankenstein*, Edgar Allan Poe's *Murders in the Rue Morgue*, and H.G. Wells' *The Invisible Man*, each sharing promotion through key art on their covers and interior photographs with the Universal motion pictures as they were released. But these were not novelizations, since they simply reprinted the original novels the new movies were based upon.

During the process of publishing movie-tie reprints, enterprising publishers came up with the notion of a contracted "novelization of the photoplay" in order to accommodate a book tie-in with a movie that hadn't been based on a previously existing novel. Thus shoppers could go into a book shop in 1928 and find a copy of *London After Midnight* by Mary Coolidge Rask, based on the Lon Chaney movie (which film, having since become infamously lost over the succeeding decades, may leave this novel as the closest approximation of the film's story extant), or, in 1932, Delos W. Lovelace's novelization of "King Kong," one of the most acclaimed novelizations which has remained in print to this day. Grosset & Dunlap, while the most prolific purveyor of the Photoplay Edition, was by no means the only one, as their success encouraged other publishers to join the bookwagon. In England, Michael Harrison (writing as "Michael Egremont") novelized "The Bride of Fran- kenstein" (published by The Queensway Press, London, in 1936; reprinted in the USA in 1976). While these "novelizations of the photoplay" weren't restricted to the science fiction and fantasy genres, these kinds of films have always seemed to generate reader interest among fans of the movies. Thus in the ensuing decades, such classic sci-fi movies were novelized as 1940's "Dr. Cyclops" (by Henry Kuttner, as a novelette; also by "Will Garth" [a house pseudonym, possibly written by Alexander Samalman] as a novel), 1954's "The Creature from the Black Lagoon" (by British writer John Russell Fearn, writing as "Vargo Statten"), and 1956's "Forbidden Planet" (by Philip MacDonald, writing as "W, J, Stuart") – all suc- cessful and popular novelists.

In the case of 1957's "20 Million Miles to Earth" (which would be Harryhausen's first movie to be published as a novelization), mystery writer Henry Slesar was contracted to novelize the film's screenplay. It was originally published in the first (and only) issue of Ziff-Davis' *Amazing Stories Science Fiction Novels*, an offshoot of their popular pulp magazine, *Amazing Stories, and* later reprinted in Forrest J Ackerman's *Spacemen* in 1964 and *Famous Monsters of Filmland* in 1965. This present edition is its first publication in book form.

Before he became renowned for his mystery stories (many of which were popularized on the original "Alfred Hitchcock Presents" TV series), Slesar wrote mystery and science fiction stories for pulp magazines, and it was this association with these pulps that resulted in his first and only movie novelization, very early in his career. "Paul Fairman was the editor of Ziff-Davis's science fiction magazines in 1957," Slesar told me in an interview for my 1995 book on novelizations, *Films Into Books*, "and for some time I'd been writing stories for him 'on order' – based upon cover art and/or titles he had already commissioned for either *Amazing* or *Fantastic*.

"This peculiar method of producing fiction resulted from the lead time required to produce cover art (usually three months ahead of publication) so the covers, with or without titles, became the 'inspiration' for Fairman's regular writers (the requirements for being a 'regular' was a degree of competence, speed, and the willingness to work cheap.) Actually, there was something exhilarating about working out a story based upon an illustration and/or title. It gave a writer a starting point, and what writer doesn't need one?"

The major challenge that faces a novelization author is expanding a film script to novel length. Most screenplays average 120 pages in length, while the average novel is between two and three hundred pages. Even writing a short novel like "20 Million Miles to Earth," which topped out at only 37,500 words (which technically makes it a novella; most regular novels average between 60,000 and 175,000 words[15] - mammoth blockbusters of the 2000s notwithstanding). To expand the film script into book form, and to describe in words nuances of character, description, and action depicted visually in the film, the author must inflate the story by augmenting character, narrative atmosphere, and "exploring the psychology and philosophy behind the characters and the events the sweep them along."[16]

In the case of "20 Million Miles to Earth," the starting point was the Williams and Knopf script, which from a literary standpoint didn't impress Slesar. "'20 Million Miles To Earth' had no stars, not in the cast and not in the reviews. It took far more effort than the pitiful renumeration would indicate," Slesar admitted. "To be candid, the screenplay was woefully lacking in depth, characterization, sense of place, or any of the other goodies that make fiction worth reading. The storyline was only wrapping paper for the special effects. When Paul Fairman gave me the assignment, the only material provided was the script, and it was soon obvious that the 'wrapping paper' would not provide enough material for a novelization, if only because of the number of words required."

Slesar discussed the adaptation with Fairman, who also considered the movie several cuts below 'B' but "expressed the hope that I would give it some flavor (I think it was that expression which made me work harder on it than perhaps warranted)," Slesar said. "Paul was a craftsman who appreciated good craftsmanship, and wanted his writer, when adapting other material, to make silk purses out of what he considered sow's ears."

The book reads quickly, with an economy of wordplay that permit the sentences to flow like the sequence of an edited movie, emphasizing dialogue while describing moments of exciting visual activity through quick bursts of written narrative, as in this scene from the climax as the soldiers confront the Ymir at the Colosseum:

But the creature was displaying a skill and tenacity that they never knew it possessed. Despite the time-worn smoothness of the concrete, despite the height of the wall, it put out its claws and gripped the old stones. It clung desperately, and began to move upwards.

In order to bring a larger sense of life to the story, Slesar tried to expand the characters and their backgrounds. "In my adaptation, everything had to be fleshed out, characters solidified (and several new ones introduced)," he explained. "In order to give the story some depth, I gave the various characters 'problems', which were exacerbated by the arrival of the Beast. Personal difficulties for the villagers; political problems for the military men assigned to Save the World. I created a 'political' situation in the hopes of giving some meaning to the simple 'ravaging monster' story, and tried to use language as a means of justifying a plotline that was only too familiar."

The novelization dispensed with the film's cautionary opening narrative and immediately set the scene by describing the fisherman of Gerra, the Sicilian fishing village, and portraying the crash of the spaceship off its shores in concise but illustrative wordplay. Slesar adds a backstory in Chapter II about Major General McIntosh and describes the purpose of the voyage to Venus, then explores Col. Calder's backstory and relates what happened on the surface of Venus, describes the strange disease that struck the crew, and depicts their fateful return to Earth in Chapter IV. Slesar also expanded the developing romance between Calder and Marisa, adding an extended epilog that follow's Dr. Uhl's final statement, concluding the developing romance between them on a more definitive note. Where the film concludes with their walking away together, Slesar brings us along to their long-awaited candlelit dinner for a more decisive resolution.

Because movies and books tell their stories differently, Slesar also had to use his narrative expertise to create tension, suspense, and shock through the selection of words, literary pacing, and punctuation to achieve a similar sense of mood in his novelization. As an example, compare how Slesar treated the first appearance of the newborn Ymir in the trailer to its descriptive rendering in the screenplay script (which is followed closely in the filmed version).

This is how the scene was described in the shooting script:

```
CLOSE SHOT  GELATINOUS MASS
   A shaft of moonlight coming through the trailer
window illuminated the odd, uncertain-shaped figure
within the mass, which is becoming clearer now, al-
though still fairly vague, and it is moving strenu-
ously as though trying to squirm out of the gelati-
nous material that encloses it.  Now a crack showed
in the wall of the material, a crack that splits
longer, wider, and then suddenly, an incredibly tiny
fist reaches out through the opening.  A fist that has
but three talon-like fingers.
```

The fist tears frantically at the opening, ripping it wider, and then something else appears - a shoulder, then a scaly back and finally a head.

The fantastic figure pauses, breathing heavily from the exertion, then resumes its struggling and a second arm with an identical three-fingered hand reaches through and rips the gelatinous material open.

Compare the script version (and, when you are able, watch the movie interpretation) with Sear's narrative, which builds dramatic intensity through punctuation and short sentence structure (you'll find this section in pages 35 of this edition).

[The moon] beams slanted through the window of the mobile home and picked out the shiny form of the gelatinous blob on the Doctor's work bench.
The strange shape inside the mass had more definition now. It began to move, to shift, to struggle.
Slowly, a crack formed in the slick surface. It grew longer, wider.
Then, something burst through the shell. A tiny fist, with three talon-like fingers.

Without the camera's point of view, Slesar opts to describe the emergence of the Ymir from the perspective of Marisa, as she enters the trailer and is startled to see the homunculus-like creature standing on a table beside her:

The peculiar sibilant noise startled her.

She whirled, and the sight of the thing on the work bench drained the blood from her face. She stifled a scream in her throat, and stared.

It was some fifteen inches high, and the moonlight delineated its grotesque reptilian shape… It waved its three-taloned hands helplessly in the air, and hissed at her as if in fright.

Thus the needs of the written word when telling a story in book meant to be read are far different from even fairly expressive instructions for the filmmakers in the script.

In today's marketplace, film novelizations and tie-ins are a routine part of a motion picture's marketing program, and they are frequently found in the wake of any popular or semi-popular film or television undertaking. Many are written by authors specializing in writing just those kinds of books. But in the early days of the 1950s, long before the advent of home video and online stream-ing, novelizations were a special way fans of a film could relive the excitement of a favorite movie once its theatrical run had ended and before its television presentation only through the retelling of the film's story in novelization form. Even then, though, books based on movies suffered under a perception that, being based on a visual medium – and a literary genre – which was often looked down upon by the literary elite, and it would be several decades before movie novelization books achieved a slightly more respectable reputation, even when written by writers of notable stature. In the 1950s, while investing their work with the same professional craftsmanship and craftsmanship they gave to their original works, writers like Slesar had little respect for the task of novelizing a movie.

"I don't claim that I extracted a worthwhile novel from the material – it's far from that (about twenty million miles)," Slesar concluded. "But at least I satisfied the urge of conscience which said: make this a decent piece of work."

All things considered, Slesar's "20 Million Miles to Earth" nonetheless remains a welcome novelette from the halcyon days of 1950's science fiction, in which barely a handful of films generated any sort of tie-in publication. That Sear's novelette reads so well is a tribute to his wordsmithing talent and his understanding of how to translate the structure of a screenplay intended for the visual medium into an engaging and exciting story to be read in the printed medium.

Randall D. Larson, 2013

Randall D. Larson has written about film, film music, and horror literature for more than forty years. A former film music columnist for **Cinefantastique** magazine, he now writes the monthly **Soundtrax** column for buysoundtrax.com. He has written liner notes for more than 120 archival soundtrack CD releases, and is the author of several books, including **Films Into Books**, the first comprehensive study of movie and TV novelizations and tie-ins (Scarecrow Press, 1995) and, most recently, an expanded Second Edition of **Musique Fantastique: 100 Years of Fantasy, Science Fiction and Horror Film Music** (Creature Features, 2012-2013). For more information, see: www.musiquefantastique.com

Portions of the Henry Slesar interview appeared previously in the author's book, **Films Into Books**.

(Endnotes)

[1] Warren, Bill, Keep Watching The Skies! The 21st Century Edition (Jefferson, NC: McFarland, 2010), p. 811

[2] Harryhausen, Ray and Dalton, Tony, Ray Harryhausen, An Animated Life (New York: Billboard Books, 2004), p. 90.

[3] Hanken, Mike, Ray Harryhausen: Master of Majicks, Vol. 2: The American Films (Los Angeles: Archive Editions, 2008), p. 193

[4] Harryhausen & Dalton, Ray Harryhausen, An Animated Life, p. 91.

[5] Harryhausen, Ray, quoted by Mike Hanken, Ray Harryhausen: Master of Majicks, Vol. 2, p. 202.

[6] Knight's first name is occasionally credited or misspelled as "Charlott"

[7] Harryhausen, Ray, Film Fantasy Scrapbook Second Edition
(New York: A S Barnes & Co., 1974, p. 50.

[8] Harryhausen, Ray, quoted by Mike Hanken, Ray Harryhausen: Master of Majicks, Vol. 2, p. 193.

[9] Mike Hanken, Ray Harryhausen: Master of Majicks, Vol. 2, p. 199.

[10] Harryhausen & Dalton, Ray Harryhausen, An Animated Life, p. 90.

[11] Schecter, David, notes to "Mighty Joe Young" (and other Ray Harryhausen animation classics) soundtrack CD (Burbank, CA: Monstrous Movie Music, 2005), p. 20. (see also Schecter's "Film Music's Unsung Hero" featurette on the "20 Million Miles to Earth" Blu-Ray (Sony, 2007).

[12] Harryhausen, Ray, Film Fantasy Scrapbook, p. 53.

[13] Mike Hanken, Ray Harryhausen: Master of Majicks, Vol. 2, p. 215.

[14] Harryhausen & Dalton, Ray Harryhausen, An Animated Life, p. 98.

[15] Unsigned Wikipedia entry, "Word Count," http://en.wikipedia.org/wiki/Word_count . Retrieved 1/28/13.

[16] John Russo, interview with this author, Oct. 1993.

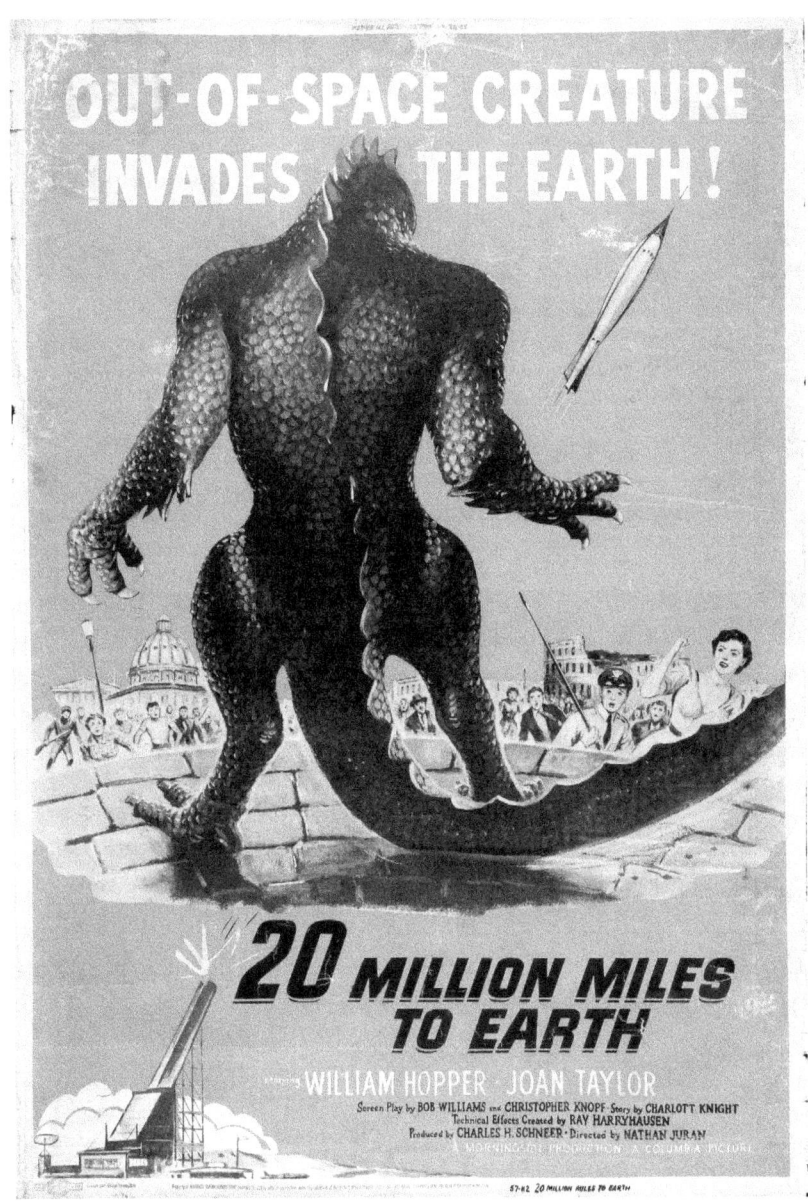

Ray Harryhausen, his Ymir model and Forrest J Ackerman

CHAPTER I

Chaos Over Gerra

THE sea loved the fishing village of Gerra. It nestled close to it, lapping on the shore; sometimes it touched the little houses of the villagers themselves. In all Sicily, no boasts were made of bigger, fatter tunny than those which wriggled in the nets of the Gerra Fishermen, and this proximity was given as the reason.

"It is because we live so close to the sea," Verrico the strongest man in the village would laugh. "The fish, they come into the house and ask for wine."

But this was brave talk, reserved for happy, carefree hours around red bottles of Marsala and the music of the concertina. When day broke over the Mediterranean, Verrico and all the rest fought hard for the daily catch in their longboats and skiffs, fought with the big nets and the long-hooked poles, and the tuna fought back with all the vigor of their breed.

It was a day no sunnier than all other days, when the fish battled no better or worse than at other times. Verrico, his thick, muscle-banded arms glittering in the sunlight, pulled on the great net, urging his partner Mondello to greater efforts. Mondello, older and shorter, and unwilling to admit to less strength in his arms than Verrico, grunting and wheezed and struggled with the heavy-leaden net. There was a third helper in the boat, too, but he was being of little service.

"Pepe!"

Mondello scowled at the boy who was twisting a small rope idly in his hands, his eyes far from the scene. "Is it your desire that the fish, they swim away? Pull upon the net, little one!

Pepe looked disgusted, in the way that only a bored eleven-year-old can. He tossed his black hair back from his forehead, and said:

"Fishnets! Many big ropes to catch a little fish!" He sighed, and his voice was jaded by too many years of monotony. "Now in

Taixas—that is where *one* little rope, he catches big cow!"

"Taixas?" Mondello grumbled. "Taixas? And what is that?"

Pepe smirked. "Ah, Mondello, you know not of Taixas? She is a big country across the sea, near America. She is where the cowboys they—"

"Silencio!"

The command came from Verrico, whose ears had been listening with amusement and whose ears now seemed to have caught some strange signal from the depth of the sea itself.

"What is it? Mondello said. Then he, too, stopped.

The men in the longboat ceased their efforts with the net, and looked out to the horizon where the blue sky met the water.

It was a sound.

It was a distant roar, and each moment grew less distant. A roar not of the sea, and unknown to the peaceful sky of Gerra. A sound reminiscent of terrible days under the *fascisti,* but somehow different. A roar that caught the ears and attention of all the fishermen of Gerra, who let the tunny escape their nets while they turned their eyes to find the source.

"Look!" Pepe shouted.

The puffy white clouds were bursting overhead, and spitting forth a silvery object so awesome that a gasp rose in unison from the men in the boats. There were flames spewing out of its tail, and its nose pointed sharply like a silver finger at the waves. Down, down it came, in a steep screaming dive, eager to meet the sea.

Then, painfully, the nose seemed to lift slightly, as if trying to avoid a head-on collision with the hard water. But whatever force guided its movements couldn't sustain the momentary lift, and the object skipped across the smooth surface of the sea like a pebble across a pond, ricocheted, struggled for altitude once more, and then careened into the depths.

In Verrico's boat, the two men and the boy watched in trembling silence, their hands moving unconsciously to cross themselves. Each was muttering brief, hurried prayers, warding off whatever devil had come tumbling from the placid sky.

Now a vast cloud of steam was rising from the fallen silver object, obscuring its view from the fishermen. For a moment, their fascinated eyes were so tightly held that they failed to see the new danger to their lives. Small tidal waves were rolling out from beneath the hissing cloud, stretching out towards the tiny fishing boats.

"Look out!" Verrico shouted, and his cry was echoed from boat to boat of the fleet. The nets were dropped, and the crews scrambled for the oars.

Verrico leaped for the tiller as a wall of churning water headed straight at their backs. Not far behind him, another fisherman slammed his tiller hard over, turning the bow into the sea. But his action came too late; the angry wave broke, and lifted the craft easily into the air, spilling its passenger into the tumultuous sea. The same action lifted Verrico's craft high, and then lowered it unharmed. He turned and looked back at the men floundering in the water, and saw another of the longboats pulling rapidly to the rescue.

Then the waters were still. And again, the fishermen turned to look at the awesome silvery thing that had fallen from the skies.

Slowly, the hissing steam was subsiding, and they saw the tail of the object projecting steeply from the water.

"It's some kind of ship," Verrico muttered. "It is an aircraft."

"Look," Mondello pointed. "A hole in the side. She cannot stay afloat long.

"Yes, I think we should—"

Mondello didn't wait to hear his next words. He was as strong and as brave as Verrico, and he was willing to declaim that fact to all Sicily, but he feared that his partner had wild and foolish thoughts in his head. He bent busily over the oars, calling to Pepe to help him. They began stroking the boat to shore, away from the scene of the disaster. The other craft in the fishing fleet were doing the same. There was no dishonor in the action; it was only common sense.

But Verrico, still looking at the aircraft, appeared to be dissatisfied.

"We stop!" he said.

The man and the boy lifted their oars.

"We go back," Verrico told them. "It is a possibility that in the aircraft there may be people."

"But, Verrico!" Mondello was through play-acting; he allowed his horror to show plainly on his face. "That is no usual aircraft. That is nothing like we have known before. There are no people in it!"

Verrico's reply was sarcastic. "Ah, but Mondello, you know this thing you say? You have been perhaps inside it?" He expanded his chest. "What are we—men of the sea, or children?

Mondello didn't answer.

"We go back," Verrico said.

They turned to the oars once more. Mondello pulled hard, and tried to keep his frightened eyes off the odd vessel in the sea ahead.

They came closer, and closer still.

"Closer," Pepe encouraged. "Closer Mondello."

"Quiet, little one!" Mondello spoke angrily. "We will get there soon enough!"

They were almost upon the thing now, close to the gaping hole in its side, the longboat bumping gently against the floating debris from the wreck. Even Verrico, whose brave features hadn't altered during the slow journey to the stricken airship, seemed no longer certain of what they were doing. When he finally spoke, his voice was hoarse.

"Pepe—the boat hook."

His eyes wide, the boy swallowed hard and lifted the hoot. Cautiously, he reached out and hooked it over the edge of the ragged hole torn into the metal of the aircraft, anchoring the boat to the crippled vessel. Verrico stepped into the gunwale, and quickly grasped the topside of the opening with his strong hands.

"You, Mondello," he whispered. "Come with me. It may be I will need your help."

"Why, Verrico? Why me?"

"Do you not boast that you are the bravest man in Sicily?"

Mondello looked miserable. Then he took a deep breath, and followed Verrico through the hole and into the darkness of the aircraft.

The floor inside was slanted by the angle of the ship. It rolled beneath their feet, and they were tipped against the metal bulkheads of the object. It was black as night in the interior of the vessel, but the reflected sunlight from the sea showed them to be in some narrow chamber, whose sides were cluttered with wires, coils, and tubing; things electronic and mysterious and frightening. Every corner of the chamber seemed to be utilized for the storage of scientific equipment or sleeping bunks. Clamped to the far wall, they could see metal cylinders of varied sizes.

One of the clamps was empty.

Verrico moved forward slowly, and Mondello's progress behind him was even slower.

Then—

"Verrico!"

"What is it?"

Mondello pointed.

There was a hand, dangling limply from behind a tangle of shattered equipment. Verrico hastened towards it, and what he saw of the man's face and body caused him to stop and curse aloud. Then, as if the curse was blasphemous even in this unholy atmosphere, the two men crossed themselves and muttered an Ave.

The aircraft shuddered.

"Verrico!"

"Steady," the younger man said hoarsely. The shuddering ceased. He stepped carefully away from the body of the man, and made his way towards a circular hatch with a wheel in its center. He reached over and turned it. There was the sound of air sucking its way into the chamber, and then a click. The hatch opened.

"Come on," Verrico said. "There may be others."

Reluctantly, Mondello followed. There were tanks in this chamber, containing strange-smelling fuel. A dangling chain on the roof swung some metal debris back and forth. The two fishermen avoided its menace, and made their way forward.

The next chamber was the last, and its scientific paraphernalia was even more over-whelming and bewildering than the first. Dials, controls, gauges, instruments, wires, tubing—Verrico's head reeled at the sight of it.

But his head cleared when he saw the man in the control chair, hunched over, his arm severely gashed, and still flowing with fresh blood.

Verrico bent over him. At first, the man's face startled him, until he realized that the ugly contours weren't his, but the face of an oxygen mask. He took off the mask, and put his ears to the man's lips.

"This man—he still lives!"

Together, they dragged the unconscious pilot of the strange aircraft back towards the open hatch. Then Verrico saw still another occupant, strapped to one of the bunks, his mask billowing noisily in erratic tempo.

"Take him out—quickly!"

Verrico hurried over to the man on the bunk as the ships frame shuddered a second time. He drew away the oxygen mask. The thin face revealed beneath it had a wasted, shriveled look that made Verrico mutter. He lifted the slight body from the bunk and carried him out behind his partner.

With Verrico's help, Mondello managed to get the injured pilot into the longboat, and then jump into the boat himself. But just as Verrico was about to leave the yawning hole in the aircraft, a third shudder took hold of the ship. This time, it threw the fisherman and his human burden against the bulkheads. Water began to slosh inside the chamber, and Pepe was shouting:

"Jump, Verrico! The aircraft sinks! Jump!"

But Verrico was determined. He tugged at the unconscious body until he was able to pass it out of the hole to Mondello's eager hand.

"Jump!" Pepe screamed, as the crippled ship trembled once more. The boat-hook slipped from the boy's grasp and Verrico knew it was now or never. He leaped, but his foot missed the drifting longboat and he plunged into the water. He swam swiftly after it, and the aircraft began vibrating mightily, its girders creaking and protesting.

They hauled him aboard just as the silver ship emitted a final, grinding groan and slowly disappeared beneath the surface of the sea.

When they rowed beyond the suction of the churning waters, they put up their oars and looked.

"There must have been more than two men in there," Pepe said brokenly.

"Almost certainly," Verrico answered. "But we could not reach them. May they rest in peace . . ."

He crossed himself. Overhead, a gull called shrilly and all was silent and serene again on the wide, blue waters of Sicily.

CHAPTER II

The Best-Laid Plans

MAJOR GENERAL A.D. McIntosh had known disappoint-
ments before. They had risen in his path like boulders on a highway,
and sometimes the tactlessness of a bulldozer.

He had begun his military career at a time when the flying ma-
chines were amusing toys, fit only for the war games of men who
dreamed a foolish dream of conquest in the air. When the world
put Billy Mitchell on trial, he had sat on the side of the prosecu-
tion. Then he had learned to dream the same dream, but almost
too late. He had served with the Air Force in World War II, when
he was already too old for combat flying. He had served in Korea,
yet never entered a jet except for transport purposes. Then his ap-
pointment to the Global Air Force came, and he thrilled again to
the challenge it raised.

And now . . .

He stood at the window of the Pentagon Building, a bull-necked, heavy-set man, his hands locked behind his back. There was emotion on the General's face, but he was reluctant to let the others see it exposed.

Dr. Judson Uhl respected the General's feelings, and waited quietly until the mood passed. He was a civilian scientist, and perceptive enough to know that even a General's uniform can cover a troubled soul.

Strangely enough, General A.D. McIntosh had been one of the last of the key men informed of the project that was known cryptically as Project XY.

It had begun as a civilian dream,, born in the great white shells of astronomical observatories, nurtured in the antiseptic laboratories of industry and government, blue-printed by civilian scientists and engineers. A vast dream indeed.

He had learned of the project on the day when an official visitor from Washington arrived at the General's headquarters, a visitor carrying sealed letters signed by the President himself.

General McIntosh frowned when he saw the man. He was the antithesis of everything military: a slumpish, weak-eyed balding man with nervous hands and an apologetic manner. His name had been Judson Uhl, and he had the title of Doctor.

"To tell you the truth," Dr. Uhl had grinned shyly, "I hardly know why I've been chosen as emissary in this matter. I'm a lot more comfortable in a laboratory, General McIntosh."

McIntosh grunted in silent agreement.

"Well, get to the point, Dr. Uhl. What's your business?"

"Rockets," the man said pleasantly.

"I see. Well, I know a little about rockets myself, Doctor."

"Not this kind perhaps, General. I'm speaking of a man-carrying rocket. One equipped to hold a crew of fifteen to twenty men, able to be launched into outer space for a trip of several months duration."

McIntosh stared at him.

"I've heard that pipe dream before, Doctor. Maybe fifty years from now, a hundred, all right. But now—"

"Yes, General," Dr. Uhl said cheerfully. "Now."

"Am I supposed to take you seriously?"

"I think so. Because the fact of the matter is this, General. Whatever talk you've heard of man-carrying rocket ships, and proposed space investigations—well, they didn't tell you the whole story. The truth is that such a vessel can be completed *now*, within a year."

"And that is the proposed plan?"

"That is the *accepted* plan, General."

McIntosh's pulse was racing. But he composed his features and said:

"A moon trip, Doctor? Or another space satellite?"

"Neither. Certain recent events have caused us to abandon our 'one-step-at-a-time' policy, General. Not only do we have the means to make an interplanetary journey—we now have the reason.

"You may have heard of the recent findings released by the Palomar Observatory. The complete details are still classified, but I can say this much. The planet Venus has revealed to our spectroscopic equipment the presence of a group of valuable minerals—essential minerals to the full development of atomic power."

The General grunted. "And these means you talk about. You really think we know enough to launch a ship to Venus? To bypass the idea of an orbital satellite? Or an exploratory moon trip?

"We know enough," Dr. Uhl said blandly. "It's been my pleasure, for the last eighteen months, to head up a scientific commission call Project XY. That commission now has the completed blueprint for the first spaceship, General. I trust it's the first.

The General looked at him sharply. "Russia?"

"We doubt it very much."

"And where does the Global Air Force fit into this scheme of yours?"

"Just where you'd think, General. The USAF will take full charge of the actual expedition; arrange the flight, man the ship, launch it, and so forth. It was the President's personal recommendation that you be the man to head up the endeavor."

The General stood up. He didn't say anything for a full ten seconds. When he did speak, the was a hushed quality in his normally gruff voice.

"I wonder if you know what this means to me, he said," he said.

"I hope it means you're happy and excited," Dr. Uhl said. "Just as I am." Then he began to bustle with the locks on his briefcase. "But we don't have time to talk about how happy we are, General. We've got work to do."

There had been a great deal of work, and never did the days of General A.D. McIntosh go by with more speed or more satisfaction. The problems of constructing the huge space vessel were well in the hands of several hundred scientists and engineers, and his advice was rarely needed on that score. But there were a thousand other matters concerning the voyage that demanded his attention. One of the most irritating was a matter that occurred seven months after the construction of the XY-21 was underway.

The finest security blanket in the history of the nation had been thrown over the entire project, but there were certain factions in the Government to whom the spaceship and its destination were no secret. One of these factions was a very powerful Congressional committee originally formed to investigate foreign aid expenditures. How its authority extended to Project XY remained a mystery to General McIntosh, who had never been politically-minded. But the effect of that authority, and the antagonism of the Senator who chairmanned the committee, became on of his gravest problems.

He met Senator Banyon at a cocktail party, a week before the official opening of the Congressional hearings, and the Senator smiled amiably and drew him aside.

Banyon was a handsome man, with silvery white hair and long sideburns. Had the General been more alert to the ways and means of political ambition, he might have recognized in the Senator a man who knew his way around a spotlight.

"This is an exciting business, General," Banyon had said smoothly. "I envy you your little project."

"Little project?" McIntosh growled. I'd hardly call it that, Senator. It may well be the most important project in the world's history."

"Ah, yes. I should know that, of course. All you spacemen use the same phrase, don't you? 'Most important event in human history . . .' That sort of excuses a lot doesn't it, General?" He smiled innocently.

"I don't know what you mean."

"I think you do. The whole concept of space travel is so awesome, so magnificent, so courageous—it's difficult for anyone, say an insignificant Congressman—to criticize the project without appearing, shall we say, reactionary?"

The General sighed, "We'll talk about it at the hearings, Senator. I came here to enjoy myself."

"Naturally, naturally. But I thought, General, that if we got to know each other a little, that might expedite matters a little. I'll make no secret as to what our line of inquiry will be next week. Money for one thing. I understand that the project cost is already well over a hundred and fifty million dollars. That's a lot of taxpaying, General. Even you can see that."

"Money isn't my business, Senator."

"No, of course not. But it's mine. These precious minerals you talk about on Venus—I wonder if *they're* worth a hundred and fifty million, General. Even if they are present in any quantity, they must still be mined and shipped. And who can say what conditions will prevail on the planet? *If* they make a successful landing. All sorts of problems intrude, don't they, Senator? He laughed pleasantly.

"There are other compensations," the General grumbled. "There's strategic value to the trip. Military value."

McIntosh was angry—more with himself than the Senator. He was on the defensive, arguing, whining. He controlled himself and said:

"Let's save it for the hearings, Senator. I'm going inside."

"Certainly, General." Banyon put his hand on McIntosh's shoulder. "Anything you say. No reason for us to personally be at odds, eh?"

The private hearings on the subject of Project XY was probably the most trying period the General A.S. McIntosh's career. The testimony of the scientists and engineers was forthright and unemotional. His own testimony on the military and tactical benefits of the Venus trip was grueling. By the end of the four-week round of questioning, it began to appear as if Project XY was in mortal danger, even before the ship was launched.

Then, just as the rumors were blackest from Capitol Hill, there were reports of high-level maneuvers from the White House—and all investigation was ended.

Senator Banyon didn't seem chagrined at the decision. He was as pleasant as ever to General McIntosh, and the General was acute enough to realize that Banyon had lost nothing in political standing.

Then a new problem arose to overshadow all others. The problem of the crew.

Some eight hundred of the Air Force's best men had been recruited in an attempt to find the seventeen that would eventually make the journey.

At the end of three months of intensive testing and examinations, Project XY found itself with only six acceptable candidates—six men who met the high standards of physical strength, coordination and endurance, intelligence and adaptability, knowledge and education, psychological aptness, and that indeterminate quality of spirit that was needed for such an endeavor.

"We must have dedicated men aboard this ship," Dr. Sharman, the chief medical officer of the project told the General. "They must believe in this voyage with all their body, their mind, and their soul. It's the only way."

The General's eyes twinkled.

"Soul, Dr. Sharman?"

"Yes, General. There are many scientists who believe more intensely in the soul of man than laymen do. They see more wonders revealed; they have more reason to have faith. Some of them give it different names, but the essential faith is there."

"That's won't solve our problem," the General said glumly. "We can't find the right men to meet the standards we've set as it is. Either we relax those standards—"

"No," Sharman said. "We can't afford to have one poor candidate aboard that ship, General; he could mean the death of the others and the death of our expedition. But I suggest we let a little human judgement into the examinations. Suppose we form a three-

Hissing, the creature stood its ground.

man committee: myself, yourself, and Dr. Uhl. We may be able to find the men."

"We'll try it," the General said. He lifted some papers from his desk. "Then here's a candidate we can pass judgement on right now. Intelligence report—excellent. Education—excellent. Psychological report—excellent. Medical report—only fair. This is an important man in an important position. The man is a botanist, a zoologist, and a physician of note; his knowledge will be very helpful.

"And the fair medical report?"

"He didn't do well in the gyroscope tests. Blacked out before the required number of g's. But that doesn't mean he won't survive the flight of course." He grinned at the Doctor. "No, Dr. Sharman, I think you'll survive it fine."

Sharman flushed.

"Thank you, General. I will plan on surviving . . ."

In the Pentagon office, General McIntosh turned around.

Without looking at the two men in the room, he strode to the huge relief map that covered one wall of the sparsely-furnished office. He glowered at it, and jammed his thumb into the middle of the Mediterranean.

"From all indications, she's splashed in somewhere right here." And added bitterly: "Twenty thousand leagues under the sea."

"Perhaps not, General," Dr. Uhl said hopefully. "It may be that Colonel Calder regained control."

"I appreciate your optimism, Doctor. But that's the way it reads. Just like that."

He traced his finger downward from Iceland across to France.

"We've got a radar blip on her just off Iceland, two hundred miles altitude. Rate of descent—" He turned to his aide. "What was it, Major Stacey?"

"Thirty-five hundred feet per minute, sir."

"Another sighting from Stillman in Marseilles. Rate of descent—still thirty-five hundred feet per minute." He jabbed at the Mediterranean again. "Sorry, Doctor—but that puts her down with the fish."

Dr. Uhl stared glumly at the map, and turned away. Quietly, his voice controlled, he said: "What makes me cry inside is that it was so close. So very, very close. They made it there. The almost made it back. And—"

The telephone rang, and the Major hurried to answer.

"Major Stacey speaking."

His face began to brighten the moment the metallic voice on the other end began to speak. He was almost grinning when he said: "Hold it! Tell the General!"

McIntosh snatched the receiver out of his hand.

"McIntosh . . . Yes? . . . Where? Is that confirmed? . . . Thank you!"

"What is it?" Dr. Uhl said, trying to hold down his exuberance.

He looked up.

"She's down off Sicily, Doctor!" He walked briskly back to the map. "Only a few kilometers off the coast of a fishing village named Gerra! Some fishermen saw it."

His blunt finger rode over the map. It searched desperately until its stubby tip came finally to rest.

"Here it is!"

He turned to them swiftly.

All right, Major. We'll need the cooperation and courtesy of the Italian Government, so get the State Department on the phone. Tell them we've got a green light from the White House, and tell them to get the Italian Embassy to clear a path for us."

Dr. Uhl grinned. "You better tell 'em we're in a hurry. Tell them to roll up their red tape and put it in a drawer and lock it up until this thing is over."

"Yes, sir!" Stacey said, grinning the while.

"One more thing," the General continued. "Tell them Dr. Uhl and I want to leave and we want to leave now. For Sicily!"

CHAPTER III

The Monster Emerges

NEVER had the fishermen of Gerra drawn such a curious catch from the sea. They gathered on the shore, buzzing and exclaiming, as Verrico and the others removed the two rescued men from the beached longboat to stretchers. The Commissario of Police, resplendent in his trim uniform, at last had his opportunity to demonstrate what a truly efficient man he was in a crisis.

"Take them to the Commune di Gerra," he said. "Quickly! And you, Mondello. Fetch the doctor! Subito!"

"Si Signore Commissario!"

Mondello turned and ran, and the police chief whipped a notebook from his hip pocket and looked at Verrico. He jotted things down.

"You were inside the wreck. Were there only these two men aboard?"

"Si. I was inside with Mondello, and we saw one more man. But he was of a certainty dead." Verrico shrugged, with great sadness. "But Signore Commissario—that ship of the air, she was so big, so vast, that surely there must have been other men inside, too."

They looked at each other, two men of great soul and understanding, and their hearts were heavy.

Neither of them noticed Pepe, who was staring at the shoreline.

At first, he saw what appeared to be a dark bit of cloth, a floating garment of some kind. There was something else bobbing beside it, a metallic object. But the bit of cloth was in Pepe's eyes, and he began to wade swiftly into the water.

He picked up the cloth thing. It was a leather jacket, still handsome and shining despite its soaking. He turned it around admiringly, covetously, and when he saw the initials USAF stenciled on the back, his face mirrored pure delight. Hurriedly, he wrung the water from the flying jacket, and looked around for other exciting discoveries in the debris of the fallen aircraft.

For a moment, he saw nothing but splinters of wood. Then, on the beach, he saw the flash of sunlight on metal, and he moved towards the object eagerly.

It was a cylinder, and the magic letters of the USAF were stamped on it, too. He picked it up; the surprising weight almost toppled him over. The end of the thing had clamps that secured the cap tightly; it resisted Pepe's young fingers.

On the shore, a new problem was coming to the attention of the Commissario. Mondello returned from his errand with bad news.

"Commissario!" Mondello was wheezing, winded from his long run. "The doctore he is not at home. He is far over at the Signora Martinelli's who is immediately to have a babino. Perhaps twins as before, who knows? And the Signore Martinelli—he is a very sick man."

Soberly, the police chief said: "That is bad. Those men are in great need of—" He stopped. "One moment! There is that old doctore from Roma, traveling with his American granddaughter. Is he still here?"

The villagers shook their heads at the question.

Verrico said: "The man with the house on wheels? Pepe would know."

He cupped his hands to his mouth and called to the boy at the water's edge. "Pepe!" Then he looked at the Commissario and chuckled. "Pepe sells him worthless shellfish. Or anything else of no value. Pepe!

The boy was startled by the call. He was just at the point of success with the cylinder's stubborn cap when Verrico's shout interrupted.

"Pepe!"

He looked wildly about for a place to hide his prize. He was forced to settle for a clump of sand, and went running to answer the call.

"Si, Verrico? You need me?"

"That old doctore from Rome who travels here. Do you know where he is?"

"Dr. Leonardo? He is camped on the Via Messina—only a small kilometer beyond the residence of Signore Greppi.

The Commissario turned to Mondello. "You are aware of this place?"

"But of course."

"Good. Beg the doctor to make haste.

Mondello nodded, and ran off once more.

In Pepe's eyes, there was relief. Now he could return to his find, to his metal cylinder with the fine letters of the American Air Force stamped across it! Who knows what wonders it held? Wonders of the great America. Perhaps even wonders of Taixas!

He picked up the object, its clamp now removed, and tilted it toward the sand.

The gelatinous blob moved slowly out of its prison, oozing its way forward with every shake of Pepe's arm, until it finally dropped softly onto the sand.

Pepe stared at it, both fascinated and repelled.

It was about fifteen inches long, bulky, and sand was clinging to its slick, wet-looking surface.

The boy tossed the cylinder aside and reached out to touch the thing with his finger. Squeamishly, he yanked it back just at the point of contact. The thing didn't react to the touch, so he tried it again.

Satisfied that the blob was inanimate, Pepe picked it up and brought it to the water. He dipped the thing in the surf to wash it of clinging sand, and looked at his prize once more.

It was smooth and semi-transparent. There was something inside, something vague and shadowy, but nothing that Pepe's young eyes could identify. He frowned at it in deep thought, and then was struck with an idea.

"Dr. Leonardo!" He said aloud.

His face radiant, he picked up the flying jacket and wrapped it cozily around the gelatinous mass. He ran off, his head whirling with exciting plans and prospects for the future.

Marisa Leonardo had long ago despaired of setting up normal housekeeping in her grandfather's trailer. It wasn't that the mobile home was cramped or uncomfortable; no, it was a perfect miniature of a cottage. She herself had picked out the furniture and accessories in Rome, not trusting her old grandfather to show good decorating sense.

"If you *must* live like a gypsy," she had told him, with an affectionate smile on her face, "then you can at least travel in comfort."

He had smiled back, and patted her hand.

"All right, little mother. But you must remember that I need working room , too. You must not clutter up my little rolling laboratory with antimacassars and potted plants."

Now, three years later, Marisa stood in the trailer and brushed her glossy black hair away from her pretty, green-eyed face, and sighed. Her grandfather's zoological equipment dominated and overran even the living quarters of the mobile house. The truck that pulled the trailer wasn't enough to hold the accumulation of fear that Dr. Leonardo traveled with. His field utensils, his test tubes, his microscope, his mounted sea specimens were everywhere.

Marisa surveyed the clutter hopelessly, but there was no strong disapproval in her glance. She could never disapprove of her grandfather or of anything that belonged to him. She owed him too much; she loved him too much.

Marisa's parents had been killed when she was eight, when the bombs were falling to destroy the remnants of Il Duce's fascist machine. Her grandfather, Dr. Leonardo, had struggled through the poverty-stricken years that followed to provide a life for himself and his grandchild. As she grew older, her skill and tenderness with the sick created a desire for medical training. Somehow, Dr. Leonardo managed the means to send the girl to America, where relatives could care for her and see to her training in the fine medical universities of the great United States. In another year, she too, would be called Doctor.

Marisa had worked hard. Her scholarship had eased the financial strain, enough to permit a long-awaited visit home. So why worry if the furniture was not so fine and polished any longer? Or if seathings were crawling beneath the unmade bed.

She laughed, and set about to straighten the rumpled sheets

In the next room, Dr. Leonardo heard the knock first. His gentle, scholarly face lifted from the study he was making of an overgrown snail. He went to the door and opened it.

"Dr. Leonardo?"

The man breathed a relieved sigh. He was stocky and strong, and there was anxiety in his face.

"I am Mondello, the fisherman. Come with me, please! Come now quickly! A great aircraft fell into the sea—a terrible tragedy—and the two men, they need you now!"

The Doctore stared blankly at him, and Marisa came in.

"What is it, grandfather?"

"I do not know yet. Slowly, my friend. Do I understand that there has been an air crash in your village, and men have been hurt?" He was trying hard to comprehend.

"Si, si! And Doctore Bomini, the only one we have, he is with the Signora Martinelli, who is about to have twins, triplets—perhaps more! Who can know?"

The Doctor shook his white head, I fear I would be of no help. I am a doctor of zoology, not medicine. But my granddaughter, it is possible—" He turned to her. "Marisa?"

She looked surprised, and Mondello turned his face eagerly towards her.

"Signorina! *You* are the doctore of people with hurts?"

"Not yet," she said. "Not for another year."

The sick look of disappointment was plain on Mondello's face. Marisa hesitated, and then said:

"All right. I'll do the best I can."

There were visions in Pepe's head, and there were sounds, too. Sounds of horses' hooves and six-shooters and the cry of the cowmen as they hooted at the scampering cattle on the plains of the great country of Taixas. A rustler with a villainous black moustache, was aiming his gun at the hero, a white-suited cowboy on an equally white horse. The hero's features were surprisingly like Pepe's own. Just as the hero's right hand darted to his gunbelt swifter than lightning. Crack! The rustler clutched his midriff and fell to the ground. Pepe came within sight of the truck and trailer, nestled snugly inside a pleasant grove, with its array of bird and animal cages hanging outside. He bare noticed the pretty young signorina hurrying out, carrying a small black bag, accompanying Mondello down the road. He had too much on his mind, and it all had to do with the strange slimy thing wrapped in the flying jacket.

"Good afternoon!"

He looked up to see Dr. Leonardo, his good friend and finest customer.

"Well, my young merchant friend. And what is it you wish to sell me today; at an exorbitant rate, I am certain. And inedible clam, perhaps?"

"Ah, Dr. Leonardo, you make one big mistake. Here I have not a clam. I have a treasure!"

The Doctor hid the amusement on his face.

"With which, no doubt, you are willing to part for very, very little money?" He gestured towards the trailer door. "Come inside, my little bandit—and we'll bargain.

Within the room, the Doctor beckoned the boy to one of the camp chairs. But Pepe stood still, clutching his treasure tightly.

"Dr. Leonardo, you are a kind man, a just man, a man of much learning. And a man of great wealth."

"A man of wealth! A professor of—" He smiled ruefully, remembering the kind of world a boy lives in. "Of course, Pepe. All things are relative. Continue."

"You have two hundred lira?"

"There is a possibility," the Doctor said solemnly, That I have such a fortune." He put his hand out towards the flying jacket. "Now may I see this new treasure of so great value."

Pepe drew back. "You have two hundred lira with you, in your purse?"

"It is a true fact, Pepe. But why is your need so great, so urgent?"

"Because. With two hundred lira. I can purchase the hat from Taixas. Please—may I have the money now?"

"The hat from Taizas?"

Pepe drew a circle around his head. "It is the hat the cowboy wears when he shoots the bandit, bang! Bang! And the man he is dead." He whipped out two imaginary guns and fired them.

The Doctor nodded. "Ah those American films. With so great a need, Pepe, you may have the two hundred lira. But I warn you—I'd better get my money's worth." His gentile face mimicked a movie villain. "Or 'I'm a-comin' after you!"

Dr. Leonardo took out his purse and peeled off two hundred

Marisa screamed in terror as the claws gripped her wrist.

lira. Pepe looked at them joyfully.

:And now what is it I have purchased—this treasure of great splendor?"

Pepe was hardly interested in that side of the transaction any longer. Carelessly, he unrolled the jacket, and put the gelatinous mass on the Doctor's work bench.

Dr. Leonardo looked at it with only mild curiosity; the sea produces many odd things.

Then he examined it closer, with increasing interest. He prodded it, turned it over. He became so absorbed in the thing that he didn't notice Pepe's hasty departure through the trailer doors.

"Strange," he said to himself. "There seems to be something inside. Something with form. But what class does it belong to? Pepe, tell me where you—"

He looked up and saw the empty room.

Hurriedly, he went to the door, shouting for the boy. Down the road, Pepe turned, his hand holding tight to the pocket where the money was.

"Si, Dr. Leonardo?"

"Please tell me! Where did you find this thing?"

"In the water, Doctor! In the sea!"

Dr. Leonardo watched him run, and he shook his white-haired head with a wry smile on his lips.

Behind him, on the work bench, the blob from the USAF cylinder quivered once, and again,

Then it was silent.

The Commune di Gerra was a building of many moods and purposes, and its hoary stones told the story of the ancient village of Gerra on the island of Sicily. It was a poor building, as its village was poor. It was old, as its village was old. Yet it was strong and sturdy, lacking in grace, but stubborn in its construction. It had weathered was and famine and the slow decay of the years, but still it stood—a home for the Mayor of Gerra, the office of the Commissario of Police and a hospital for the sick.

On the hospital floor, in one large barren room, there were three cots. One was empty. The other two held the unconscious bodies of the men taken from the stricken aircraft.

The younger of the pair, his wounds swathed in professional bandages around his head and arm, lay breathing normally.

The other man was less fortunate. An oxygen tank had been placed near his head, and a small face mask covered his mouth.

Marisa Leonardo picked up his limp wrist and tried his pulse again. She listened implacably to the sound of his heavy, erratic breathing, and put the wrist back on the bed. It dropped like a weight.

Then she looked into the man's contorted face, and her expression was puzzled. Not even her worst dreams had featured such a mangled, tortured face as this. What had happened to the man? What nightmare was upon him?

A grunting sound came from the other cot. She got up and went to the younger man. His eyes were shut, but his head was beginning to move on the pillow. She tried his pulse, and at her touch, his eyes struggled open.

She said: "I know. You want to know where you are. Well, you're in Sicily, in a village called Gerra."

"Gerra?"

"Southern Sicily. A fishing village." She dropped his wrist and smiled professionally.

"About where we figured," he said vaguely. Then his expression changed, and he strained to sitting position.

"The others? How are they?"

She answered gently.

"I'm told that your aircraft is at the bottom of the sea. Whoever else was on it . . ." She watched him fall back wearily. "Except, of course, this gentleman here. And his condition is critical—very critical."

The man looked at the other cot. When he saw its occupant, he forced his feet over the side of the cot.

"I'm sorry," Marisa said, restraining him. "You're in no condition to—"

"Let me alone!" He pushed her away rudely, clutching the side of the cot for support. He got up weakly and tottered towards the other bed.

"Please, you mustn't—"

But there was determination on the young man's lean intense face. He bent over the unconscious man and put his mouth to his unheeding ear.

"Doctor! he shouted. "Dr. Sharman!"

Vainly, Marisa tried to pull him away, but he was strong and stubborn.

"I must ask you to leave this man alone. He's extremely ill—"

"Please! Dr. Sharman, can you hear me?"

"If you don't stop, I'll call for help—"

The man whirled on her, his face infuriated. There was a depth of anger in his eyes that she wasn't used to seeing, a grim preoccupation that transcended everything else.

"Listen, nurse, leave me alone! I'm in no mood to—"

"I'm *not* a nurse!" she said loudly. "I'm a doctor—or almost a doctor—and this man may be dying!"

The young man took a deep breath, as if fighting for patience. "All right, almost-a-doctor. Do you know what's wrong with him?"

"No—not exactly."

"Well, I do! I know what's wrong with him, and I know it's fatal. Eight of my crew have already died of the same thing. Now if you must stay here, stand still and be quiet. Understand?"

Marisa's eyes widened, and she gasped. Just slightly, her arm raised as if it involuntarily desired to strike the insulting young stranger across his face. She glared back at him, but he wasn't interested in her reaction. He was bending over the dying man, calling "Sharman! Dr. Sharman! Can you hear me?

Then the man moved.

His movement was slight, but his young friend became excited, and shouted louder.

"Doctor!"

The words that came from the distorted lips were hardly audible.

"Are we . . . are we going to make . . . make it back?"

"We *are* back! We're on Earth!"

"The specimen! Is it all right?"

"I—I don't know. We crashed into the Mediterranean. I suppose everything went down with the wreck." He paused. "The others are dead.

The man he called Sharman shut his eyes tightly. He tried to speak once more, but there wasn't enough breath in his lungs. His hand inched upwards, making its way into his coat. It emerged with a notebook.

"Make them . . . make them find it . . .my notes . . ."

He began to gasp for breath. Marisa, watching with hypnotized eyes, came closer.

"How long can it live?" the young man was saying. "How long can it live in the cylinder, Dr. Sharman? I've got to know. It's our only hope."

There was no answer. Swiftly, the man grabbed for the oxygen face mask and slapped it over his friend's mouth. The breath came easier, but still faintly.

"Please," Marisa said, almost in a whisper.

He looked up, all the anger dissipated. "It's okay," he said. "I'll be all right."

"You're suffering from shock and exhaustion. You better lie down."

"Sure," the man said casually, and then almost collapsed on the cot.

Briskly, Marisa opened the bag on the table and removed a hypodermic needle.

"What were you talking about? What specimen? What fatal disease? I don't understand any of this."

"You don't. And you won't."

She made an exasperated noise. "You make a wonderful patient. Courteous. Cooperative. Informative. Altogether a joy and a pleasure to have around."

She lifted the needle. "This'll give you pleasant dreams. If you're capable of them."

She was drawing it away when the sudden silence in the room caught their attention. For a moment, she looked baffled, and then realized that the sound of Sharman's erratic breathing had ended.

She turned her head and looked at the younger man. There was no surprise on his face. She got up hastily and went to Sharman's side, reaching for his wrist.

"He—he's dead."

"I know."

She was shocked by the answer. Her voice was hard when she spoke to him again.

"Do you mind explaining all or some of this?"

"I'm sorry . . ." His voice was thick with the effects of the drug. "But I can't . . ."

"Can't? Or won't?"

He yawned widely. "Both . . ."

His head rolled over on the pillow.

Marisa walked over to him, her features moving in anger and frustration. She began to put her instruments back in the bag, but stopped again to look at her patient. He was deep in a drugged sleep, his breathing regular, his face relaxed. His features were altered now, no longer contorted by wrath. Marisa's eyes softened. He was actually handsome, and somehow vulnerable in sleep. She moved to a table piled high with blankets and shook one out. She covered him tenderly, tucking it in around his shoulders. Then she brushed back the tumbled brown hair from his forehead.

It was the same moon outside.

It had shone softly over Sicily when Marisa was a child. It had followed her to America, silvery-white and perfect over the campus of the medical school. But tonight, hanging low over the trees of Gerra, the moon seemed brighter and more romantic than Marisa Leonardo had ever known it. She followed its path down the road that led back to her grandfather's trailer, and there was a small smile on her pretty face.

But the moon wasn't shining for her alone. Its beams slanted through the window of the mobile home and picked out the shiny form of the gelatinous blob on the Doctor's work bench.

The strange shape inside the mass had more definition now. It began to move, to shift, to struggle.

Slowly, a crack formed in the slick surface. It grew longer, wider.

Then, something burst through the shell. A tiny fist, with three talon-like fingers.

Strangely Marisa wasn't tired. Her mind was active, thinking rapidly, puzzling over the strange words she had heard spoken inside the Commune di Gerra. She knew that the two rescued in the hospital ward were members of the United States Air Force, and their mission had been one of danger and importance. But what had caused so many deaths among the crew? And what unknown plague had tormented the dead man's features?

With a sigh, she put down her surgical bag and began to shrug off her jacket.

The peculiar sibilant noise startled her.

She whirled, and the sight of the thing on the work bench drained the blood from her face. She stifled a scream in her throat, and stared.

It was some fifteen inches high, and the moonlight delineated its grotesque reptilian shape. It's incredibly long, lizard-like tail swished behind it; its head was nightmarish, like that of a medieval dragon's. It waved its three-taloned hands helplessly in the air, and hissed at her as if in fright.

Marisa stood rooted to the spot, watching the creature's frightened eyes. It began to back away, as if fearful of an attack. Her hand went out automatically and flicked the light switch.

The creature jumped at the sudden burst of light in the room.

"Grandfather," Marisa whispered. "Grandfather!"

There was no sound behind the curtained aperture.

"Grandfather!"

This time, Dr. Leonardo responded to the urgency in her voice. He came out from behind the curtain, clutching his dressing gown.

"What is it, Marisa?"

He looked in the direction of her round-eyed gaze, and saw the creature on the bench. It hissed towards him and backed up even further. For a long time he did nothing but stare, and then his zoological training and instinct replaced any panic in his actions.

"My gloves," he said. "Where are my gloves?"

"Under the bench—"

The thing hissed again, a sound of warning, as the Doctor groped for his protective gloves. He picked them up hastily, slipped them on, and then placed his fingers carefully on the edge of the bench, only inches from the creature. Slowly, his hands raised towards it, and perspiration gleamed on the Doctor's forehead.

"Be careful," Marisa said.

The creature hunched its shoulders, its razor-sharp claws up-lifted. But it didn't resist the old man's touch as the Doctor's fingers closed around its scaly body.

He lifted it up, and Marisa recoiled.

"What is it? Where did it come from?"

"Pepe," the Doctor said. "The little fisher-boy." He put it down again. "I have never seen anything like this. There is no scientific record of such a creature."

Now he was all man of science, his voice calm and professorial. He picked up a pencil from the bench and pointed to the creature's anatomy. She spoke to his granddaughter as if to a zoological college.

"See? The torso resembles that of a human being. The head—I cannot classify the head. The tail is reptilian and observe the articulation of the legs." He straightened up. "But where it came from—"

He stopped when he saw the remnants of the gelatinous mass still on the work bench. He prodded it with his finger, and realized at last its true significance.

It was an egg.

"Pepe said it came from the sea. But still I do not know—" He reached for the creature again. "Marisa, open the empty cage in the truck. Make haste!"

The girl went to the door of the trailer, and her grandfather followed with the creature in his grip.

They made their way to the truck parked beside the mobile home, and Marisa threw back the tarpaulin that covered its end. There were cages of varying sizes inside, and in all but one, small animals and birds scurried frantically.

The empty cage stood about five feet tall. She swung open the wire door.

"A soft cloth," Dr. Leonardo said. "We must cover the floor of the cage. It is too hard, too rough."

Marisa provided the cloth for the bottom of the creature's new home, and Dr. Leonardo placed him gently inside. He closed the cage door, latched it securely, and they stood off to stare wonderingly at the odd beast. It began moving about uneasily, hissing and emitting sharp, eerie cries. The sound was grating, but filled with a strange fearful longing. Undefinable yet erudent.

Dr. Leonardo shivered in spite of himself.

"So ugly," Marisa said quietly. "And so very frightened." Her voice was pitying. "Poor little thing . . ."

"You are indeed your mother's daughter," Dr. Leonardo said tenderly. "Always having pity for even the meanest of God's creatures. I must confess—even I could not call this a 'poor little thing.' There is something of Hell about the beast . .."

He put his thin arm about her shoulder, and they returned, confused and fearful to the trailer.

While Bob Calder, alone with the dead body of Doctor Sharman in the Rome Hospital room, stared dully at the wall and relived the chain of events that had caused all this to be the strange sequence that was responsible.

CHAPTER IV

The Things That Went Before

THERE were eagles on Robert Calder's shoulders.

He was young for the rank, but he was in a young man's business. He had started as a child to yearn for the freedom of the air, the upper sky, and then space. But he had been luckier than General McIntosh, his commanding officer. His dreams had become realities. From box kites to model aircraft, from home-made gliders to circus stunting in the Flying School of Kansas, from the P-40's of World War II to the Thundering jets of Korea, Calder had known the sky first-hand.

Then he started having bigger dreams—dreams as big as the blue bowl that covered the night sky. A vision of winking stars and mysterious alien worlds, of a flying mission greater and more daring than Man had ever attempted before. He had had few hopes to see that dream come true in his lifetime, until the sudden arrival of orders from the headquarters of the Global Air Force. It was then he learned that other men shared the dream, and were willing to work for its reality.

He never forgot his first interview, when he learned the requirements of a crewman on the first spaceship. His interviewer was a gentle-faced, balding man with nervous hands. His name had been Dr. Judson Uhl.

"How much do you weigh, Major?"

"Hundred and seventy-five pounds."

"Think you need all that weight? You're what, five-eleven, six?"

"Six-one, sir."

"Drawback right there," Dr. Uhl said casually. Our ideal spaceman would be a midget about so high and forty pounds in weight."

"Sorry, sir. I'm not a midget."

"Yes, so I see. But you can understand our point. Every less ounce of payload will help greatly to get this ship of ours off the Earth. And how old are you, Major?"

"Twenty-six."

"Too bad. We'd prefer it if you were eighteen. But then, you probably wouldn't have the know-how or education we require. It's all a matter of balancing out the various factors, you see."

"So far, I feel like a total loss."

Dr. Uhl smiled. "That can't be decided until after a series of test are made. Physical, mental, and psychological. We're going to find out your reaction to weighing nothing or weighing five hundred pounds. We're going to test your orientation to loneliness, to no-gravity, to a lot of other things."

"Sounds rugged."

"It will be, Major. You'll have to want this thing awfully bad in order to go through with the examinations. But let's face it, Major Calder. Standards on paper are one thing. Human judgement is another. But let's say you come through with flying colors. Let's say you make the grade. Do you know the consequence of passing our tests?"

"Sure I do." He stiffened. "Space."

"Yes space. Sounds good, sounds grandiose. But you may find it full of a lot of dirty, unpleasant problems. While you're waiting around for your examinations to begin, think them over. The little things, Major. The little things, Major. The problems of food and drink in a weightless ship. The possibility of sterility caused by cosmic radiation out in the void. The problem of excessive carbon dioxide in the air you breathe; your own breath poisoning you. Think of the problems of personal hygiene of living and breathing in a space suit. Think about waste elimination. All a lot of grimy, dirty problems, Major. Think about them. We have.

"You trying to scare me off, Dr. Uhl?"

"Not in the least. I'm trying to give you a portrait of the future, Major Calder. Believe me, you won't have enough time in the next few weeks to think these things over. So start now. If anything really troubles you, come to me and we'll talk things over. Maybe I'll ease your mind—or maybe I won't."

He grinned, and unfolded his arms.

"By the way, what's your aim in this project of ours? What job do you want to fill?"

"Only one," Calder said. "Pilot."

"That's a tall order. We plan to have only one pilot Major. Each crew member will be taught the rudiments of flying the ship, in case of emergency. But we still plan only one official pilot. And he'll be commander of the expedition as well."

"I know that."

"And that's your only aim. You've got a lot of competition."

"Yes, sir. But that's the job I want."

Dr. Uhl turned his back.

"That's all, Major.

He was still smiling when Calder was out of the room. He knew his man.

Calder's life had changed drastically that day. He was subjected to a series of grueling examinations that made OCS training seem like an ROTC picnic. He almost flunked them, too, during a psychological tryout that caught him unprepared, and revealed a significant flaw in his makeup.

The inquisitor had been a sour-faced Colonel with red-tape mentally written all over him. From the moment the interview began, Calder was on edge.

The Colonel said: "Flyboy, huh?"

"Pardon, sir?"

"I said flyboy, glamour pants, plane jockey. You heard me, Major.

Calder said nothing, but his lean face began to redden.

"Bet you think you're a privileged character, don't you? Thing that Air Force patch gives you special rights. You're too good for us earth-bound joes, aren't you, Major?"

"I don't see what you mean, sir."

"You know damn well what I mean. I met your type before, Major. Cocky young punks. Make Captain at twenty-one, Major at twenty-four. Got the world by the short hairs. Now you're angling for a real cozy assignment. Real movie-star stuff. Spaceships. Buck Rogers—"

Calder was flushing so hard that he looked ready to explode. He let out a gust of air and said: "Are you kidding? I didn't ask for this assignment—"

"That mean you don't want it?"

"Sure I want it! Think I'd let 'em push me around this way if I didn't. Did you ever sit in that centrifuge gadget of theirs, Colonel? That's no picnic—sir."

"Why do you want it? So you can sell your story to the movies? Big hero stuff?"

"No!"

The Colonel just sneered.

"All right, maybe I do!" Calder shouted. "I don't know myself! But what the hell's the difference? We've all got reasons for everything we want."

"You realize how slim your chances are? Of surviving such a trip?"

"Sure. But I know how to handle myself. If this thing can fly, I can fly it."

"Pretty sure of yourself, aren't you? And maybe a bit immature?"

Calder stood up, and the chair he was sitting on scraped back so hard that it thundered against the wall.

"Listen *sir,*" he said hotly. "If you want to talk, talk. If you want to poke around in my private life, and ask me if I like girls, and stuff like that—ask. But if you want me to fly that crate of yours—sir—"

"That's enough!" the Colonel snapped. "Stand at attention, Major!"

Calder was shaking with rage, but stiffened at the command.

When he walked out of the room, his face was glum.

Later that day, he received orders to report to General McIntosh's quarters. He went down the corridor slowly, trying to delay the inevitable bad news.

The General's salute was absent-minded, his eyes fixed on Calder's face.

"Received a note about you, Major. Not a good report. Seems you have a hot temper."

"Yes, sir."

"A hot temper has its place, Major. In combat, maybe. But for the mission we have in mind—" He sighed, and got up to walk to the window of the office. The night sky was clear, and the stars sharp and brilliant.

"I'm sorry, sir," Calder said. "I realize now that I was being deliberately baited. But I didn't like his slurs about the Air Force."

The General turned to him, amused. "You trying to butter me up, Major?"

"No, sir," Calder flushed. "It's just that—well, I love flying, sir."

The General nodded. "So do I, Calder. So do I. But I've never been anything more than a glorified passenger. You're been lucky. You can be even luckier, if you really wanted to be."

"I do, sir."

"This ship we plan to launch will require seventeen crewmen and one pilot. One pilot, Calder. That man is very important to us. He must be as perfect a man as we can find."

"Yes, sir."

"He must be able to keep his head at all times. He will be performing an unprecedented feat. He will meet conditions no man has met before. A perfect man, Calder."

"Yes, sir," the Major said unhappily.

Then the General was grinning.

"But I doubt if there is such an animal on Earth, Major Calder. Flawless. Emotion-proof. Humans aren't as perfect as the stars."

Calder's heart thudded, but still he said nothing.

"The final decision on the man awaits the recommendation of three men. Dr. Uhl, the civilian scientist in charge, is one of them. Another is Dr. Sharman, our medical officer. Both have already made up their minds, so the outcome rests with the third man. Myself."

"Yes, sir."

The General walked towards him and put his hand on Calder's shoulder.

"Fly it for me," he said softly. Fly it for me, Major."

Two months later, before the sun had risen over the hills of Nevada space station, the XY-21 was poised and ready.

Thunder began to roll over the mountains, thunder man-made and rich with promise of the things to come.

The huge spaceship shuddered, and its rocket fire spilled over the ground beneath it. Slowly, it raised itself from the giant grip of the earth, and slowly it climbed upwards with gathering speed. Then, as if flinging off the shackles of gravity, the vessel ripped into the clouds overhead, tearing at the heavens with its sharp-pointed nose. At last, only the faint glow of its exhaust could be seen by the spectators below.

Inside the ship, Robert Calder, now with a Colonel's insignia sewn to his ballooning gray space-clothing, lay flat in the chair that was to be his home for many weeks ahead.

The sixteen members of the ship's crew were similarly prisoners of the iron force of the ship's acceleration. The force crushed their bodies, squeezed their hearts and lungs, flattened the contours of their faces. *Brennschluss* was reached in two interminable minutes, and then the acceleration began again, with a new supply of atomic fuel blazing in the rocket's underbelly.

Some came out of the acceleration coma without difficulty; others took many hours before they could accept the new horror of the journey weightlessness.

Their minds hazy, their fingers not behaving as their training demanded, with movements awkward and slow, their behavior irrational, their tempers short . . . weightlessness was the true horror. But even these were finally conquered, conquered by months of pre-conditioning in the Earth laboratories below.

But despite all the preparation, there were problems. Even the ingenious devices created by Dr. Uhl and the others couldn't recreate the identical conditions of space-flight to the nth degree. The true answers to man's reaction would be found only in space. And Colonel Calder found them.

First there was Jensen, the hard-muscled blond boy with the incredible head for calculus and the unblinking eyes of a cobra. He had been the quietest of all the candidates for the XY-21, and his quietness had caused concern among the psychologists. But they had given him the decision, reasoning that his lack of gregariousness was well compensated by his sober, intelligent outlook on life, his physical stamina and his keen mathematical brilliance.

But Jensen went wrong in space.

At first, he reacted to the zero gravity of the ship by a surprisingly gay attitude. Of all the crew, it was Jensen who grinned widest when pencils floated and poured coffee remained in a pulsating ball of liquid in the cabin. He had laughed, and talked of the free-fall sensation as if it were a great joke. Later, Colonel Calder cursed himself for not realizing that Jensen had laughed too much.

On the fourth day of the trip, Calder woke to find Dr. Sharman's hand on his shoulder.

"What is it?"

"It's Jensen. Monkeyshines. Or maybe something else—"

Calder clamped his magnetic shoes on the floor beside his bunk, and looked in the direction of Sharman's troubled eyes. He saw Jensen floating near the top of the ship's "ceiling," pushing his way along the roof with his fingers, giggling foolishly.

"He took off his magna-shoes," Sharman told the commander. "Acting like it's a great game. Only there's more to it than that, Bob. Jensen; he's no schoolkid you know—"

"Jensen!" the Colonel barked. "Grab on to a ladder and get down. That's an order."

Jensen only chuckled. "Come on up, Colonel. Enjoy yourself."

"I said it's an order, Jensen—"

"Hey, Colonel, you're upside down. You're the one that's topsy-turvy, Colonel not me. It's all a matter of viewpoint. How about that Colonel?" He laughed in his throat, and the laugh went on a long time.

"Haffner," Calder said to the first engineer. "Go up and pull him down. Dr. Sharman, you get a sedative ready."

Hensen fought off the engineer's approach. It took three men to get him under control, and four to hold him down while the chief scientist applied the point of a hypodermic to his arm. They rubbed his flesh, trying to get the sedative to circulate in the weightless atmosphere. Finally, Jensen relaxed, and fell into a labored, delirious sleep.

When he awoke, Jensen was his silent self again. Colonel Calder was never to tell Jensen's family that the blond man had never spoken again. When he died on Venus, he went silent to the grave in that distant planet.

There were other personal mishaps before the XY-21 made landfall on the cloud-shrouded planet that was their destination.

Bailey, the youngest member of the crew, whose cheerfulness had inspired them all during the dreary weeks of the trip, was stricken by a strange fever for which they had no palliative. He had been one of the first to die when the poisonous vapors of Venus infiltrated their breathing apparatus. Key Kyoto, the young Chinese physicist, had gone berserk just before the landing, and had to be restrained forcibly. Mason and Cardell, who had begun an abiding friendship during the days of examination on Earth, suddenly began quarreling bitterly over trifles, and refused to speak to each other again, Even Manson's death on Venus didn't soften Cardell's heart; he continued to curse him on the return flight, and died in the Mediterranean Sea without forgiveness forgiveness for his friend.

But despite all, the day came when the planet Venus hovered in the viewscope—and for a moment, harmony had been restored on the ship.

The landing had gone far more smoothly than they had been anticipated. The heavy clouds that blanketed the planet were considered to be the major hazard of the entire flight. Using infra-red sighting equipment, they had scouted the globe for a safe surface area, and the descent had been made with unexpected ease. For a moment, it almost seemed as if the yellow clouds of Venus had parted, like the Red Sea of Moses, to permit their entry on the silent, sandy world. The event had an almost mystical quality, and Colonel calder found himself uttering a prayer of thankfulness when the rocket's fire carved out a landing surface beneath them, and the ship came to rest.

Excitement crackled in the atmosphere of the vessel as they prepared for debarkation. Suddenly, everyone was helpful and happy; even the tight-lipped Jensen had an added gleam in his eyes as he strapped on the breathing apparatus that had been provided for them. Mason and Cardell forgot their feud for the minutes before the hatch opened on Venus. Key Kyoto seemed calm once more, and Bailey's fever was not so debilitating.

Dr. Sharman repeated the brief orientation speech that had been heard a dozen times since the voyage began.

Then Colonel Calder turned the wheel that opened the hatch.

They came out in single file, with Calder having the duty, the honor, and the danger of stepping forth first on the spongy , sandy terrain of the planet. He described his impression later as: "A yellow-reddish mist all around us, like a fire burning on a foggy night. No stars visible. Mist everywhere; mist around your ankles so that you couldn't see your feet. It was cold and damp, too; even through the spacesuit you could feel the cold clinging to your skin. The ground seemed to be of sand, yet it felt wet and mossy, spongy somehow. You were never really sure of your footing, and yet you never lost your balance.

The first words spoken on the planet were those of Shuster, the chief geologist of the expedition. He flicked his radio switch and said:

"Dis mus' be de place."

It was good to hear the responsive laughter of the men despite his nervous overtones.

Calder said: "Looks like our big problem might be darkness.

When we bivouac around the ship, we'll have to break out the electric torches first thing. Then if it doesn't brighten up, I think we'll have to erect some kind of lighting system around the ship, so we can find it at all times. Dr. Sharman—"

"Yes, Colonel?"

"Would you take charge of setting that up?"

"Yes, sir?"

"Okay. We won't do any exploring right now. Every man knows his duties; let's get the right supplies unloaded. Keep everything close to the ship, and don't anybody decide to wander off. Any man found more than twenty yards from the XY gets a summary court-martial."

There was a great deal to do in the next eight hours. The crew members set about their jobs with little waste motion and much enthusiasm. Dr. Sharman and the two others set up the portable generator and a string of powerful floodlights outside the ship, and their cheerful glow helped dispel some of the gloom that surrounded them.

"Looks good," Mason drawled. "Now we can find the ship fine, Colonel. Only question is—now anything on Venus can find *us.*"

"I wouldn't worry," Calder said. "If there was intelligent life on the planet, we'd have heard from them by now. We didn't exactly sneak in, you know."

"Well suppose it's unintelligent," Mason said "But *mean.*"

Calder laughed, and returned to work.

It was on the second day of cautious exploration, when the ring had been widened to include some fifty yards around the ship that the short-circuit occurred.

Four men were guarding the XY-21 while the others went about their varied duties. None of the four realized what was happening until the sparks began to fly from the power lines outside and the strangled, terrorized shriek came to startle them into action.

"Holy catfish!" Shuster said, looking at the victim of their unwitting trap. "Get a look at *that* baby! Must be eight feet tall!"

"And ugly," Bailey said. "Look at that tail—absolutely prehensile. And that face—"

"Must have been electrocuted," another crewman suggested. "Wandered into the power lines; might have been trying to eat the damn things. But the voltage wasn't very high—"

"Wait until the Colonel gets a load of this. Hey—do you suppose the thing's intelligent?"

"I doubt it," Shuster said, shaking his head. "It's too damn *ugly*"

"Oh, I dunno, Shuster. You're no beauty, but I hear you're pretty smart."

"Knock it off. Hey, let's get the circuit fixed before our boys get lost in that crazy desert. We'll worry about our monster friend later."

Later, it was Dr. Sharman who was most concerned with the examination of the alien beast who had stumbled into the camp. His excited study of the creature occupied their attention for the next five hours on the planet. But their attention was diverted shortly afterwards, when young Bailey fell in a dead faint.

Calder had him brought into the ship, assuming that the fever had come upon him again. But there was little fever. Baukey's breath was labored, his voice choked, his pupils dilated. And there was an odd tinge to the sputum and blood samples that Dr. Sharman took from the youth's body.

He drew Colonel Calder aside.

"I don't like the color-change, Bob. I can't explain it, but I suspect some kind of poison in Bailey's system."

"Poison? Maybe he's eaten some spoiled ration. Maybe he got careless and sampled some of the local vegetation—"

"I don't think so. But we'll run a check on the food stores. If there's something wrong with it—" He looked grim.

A thorough check was made of the food supplies and no trace of contamination was detected.

The exploration went on.

Twelve hours after Bailey's faint, the boy gasped out something about his family, and died in Shuster's arms.

They buried him in the spongy sands of Venus. Colonel Calder presided at the burial ceremony, and consecrated Bailey's remains to God and to Man's aspiring spirit.

Then the poison spread.

It seemed to come upon the men all at once. Almost within an hour of each other, the crew felt the sudden surge of dizziness and nausea; the strange combination of exhilaration and depression; the clutching pain at their hears and lungs. One by one, the stricken men were led back to the ship by those whose attacks had been mild.

And one by one, in as many hours, eight men of the XY-21 died, twenty million miles from home.

"That settles it," Calder told the numb group of survivors inside the ship. We're going to have to cut the voyage short. There are only nine of us left now; that means each one of us will have to perform extra duties on the return voyage. We can't risk losing another man. I know there's still a lot we want to do here—I know that Dr. Sharman is hardly satisfied with the small amount of territory we've been able to cover. But for the good of this entire enterprise, I'm ordering this ship back."

Dr. Sharman stood up.

"We will not use the word failure. We have collected many samples. We have mineral, botanical, and geological specimens. And we have the egg of the creature that stumbled into our power lines. We will not use the word failure, Colonel.

Glumly, they set about their duties, readying the XY-21 for the return journey.

No one looked back at the eight unmarked graves, already blanketed by the mist and shifting sand. But Shuster said:

I wonder if God knows where Venus is?"

"Sure he does," Calder answered. "He'll know they're there. And they'll get special attention. Take my word for it.

An hour later the rockets of the XY-21 were exploding again.

And a few weeks later crippled by a meteor strike, the ship returned home—only to disappear forever into the sea and with it untold months perhaps years of progress.

CHAPTER V

The Empty Cage

THE day broke, serenely as ever, over Sicily.

Marisa listened to the familiar sounds of bird and animal chatter, as her grandfather's specimens he had collected greeted the day.

Then:

Marisa! Marisa!

It was Dr. Leonardo's voice, calling excitedly but without alarm. She got up quickly and opened the door of the trailer.

"Yes, Grandfather?"

"Come here!"

She stepped out of the trailer and followed her grandfather to the truck. He was pointing to the cage that had received the creature from the egg the night before.

"Observe, mi cara," he said. "Observe our friend this morning."

She looked, and the sight startled her.

The creature had grown.

"It's impossible!" she gasped. "He—he's twice the size. He's almost three feet tall!"

"Yes. And in a few hours . . ."

"It's unbelievable!"

The creature hissed at them, its reptilian tail swished against the soft clothe at the bottom of the cage. Its ugly eyes were fixed on the girl.

"Just thin!" Dr. Leonardo said. "This is a genuine phenomenon. Something *suis generis*. Think what will be said when I bring this strange creature to the Museo Zoologico in Roma!"

He started to move away. Marisa said: "Where are you going?"

"To the village. To learn from the fisher-boy where in the sea it was that he found our friend."

"Grandfather—"

"Yes, my child?"

She shook her head, her eyes still adhered to the dragon-like head of the creature.

"Nothing . . ."

The fortress was a master-work of the pioneer's art. Built sturdily of sand near the prow of an overturned fishing boat, and at least two feet high, it was perfect for defending the plainsmen against Indian attack. Especially when its chief (and only) occupant was so skilled with the six-shooter, and were such an awe-inspiring cowboy hat.

"Pow! Pow!" Pepe's wooden gun picked off another savage. "Pow! Pow! Pow!" They were biting the dust all around him. He turned towards the beach where Verrico, Mondello and the others were preoccupied with the hanging of the nets, wanting them to notice his talent and bravery.

But what he saw caused his face to change. Dr. Leonardo! His hand went anxiously to the cowboy hat on his head. Was the old man coming to ask for his two hundred lira? Had he been disappointed with his purchase?

Pepe didn't wait to find out. He crawled around the other side of the boat's hull, holding fast to his hat from Taixas, ducking out of sight.

The Doctor was speaking.

"Salutos, Verrico, Mondello. You can perhaps inform me of the whereabouts of the boy, Pepe?"

"Pepe?" Mondello snorted. "He is over there, playing like a Taixas cowboy—" He looked at the fortress, now deserted to the Indians. "Ah, he has gone! Yet he was here a moment ago."

Verrico said: "I shall see him tonight, Doctore, and tell him to seek you out tomorrow."

Dr. Leonardo shook his head. "No. Tomorrow I shall not be here. Today Marisa and I are on our way to Roma. But grazie. Addio. Do not trouble any more."

"Addio, Doctore."

From his hiding place. Pepe watched with satisfaction as Dr. Leonardo strode sadly away. Now his hat was safe! He touched it admiringly, and was about to return to his fortress, when the sound of airplane motors in the blue sky caught his ears.

He looked upwards, and his mouth opened in wonder at the sight of the Navy seaplane dropping gracefully to the water, landing in a wash of white foam.

How wonderful life was becoming! Pepe thought. In so few hours, he had seen an amazing giant aircraft dive forever into the sea. He had seen real flying men from the great United States Air Force, and had recovered one of their jackets for his very own. And most important, he had found a treasure in the sea worth two hundred lira, the price of the cowboy hat from Taixas. And now—

From the direction of the town, a dust-caked jeep was driving swiftly towards the shoreline. The Commissario of Police was sitting stiffly beside the driver. When his jeep halted, he got out and looked towards the landed plane.

Pepe crouched behind the boat, which had suddenly become a huge boulder in the middle of Death Valley. A villainous snarl crossed his sun-browned face, and he loaded his wooden gun from an imaginary gunbelt. He lifted it, took careful aim at the seaplane, and—

"Pow! Pow!"

It was a direct hit, although the two men climbing out of the plane and onto the wharf ladder, didn't seem effected by Pepe's bullets. Nevertheless, the boy was satisfied with his day's work. He stuck his gun into his holster, hitched his pants, and walked off.

The Commissario stepped forward.

"May I introduce myself, General. I am Signore Unte, Commissario of Police in Gerra. From the Governo in Roma, I have received a telegramma. I am to cooperate with you, and assure you that my facilities are yours."

General McIntosh put out his hand. "Thank you, Signore Unte. And this is Dr. Uhl."

"How do you do," the Doctor said.

"The honor is mine." The Commissario seemed to bow to the General. "If you will but accompany me, I will take you to your Colonel Calder."

McIntosh couldn't conceal the quick look of worry that crossed his square, heavy-jawed face.

"Is he—he's not badly hurt, is he?"

"Pray rest assured, General. He recovers rapidly."

They drove off in the jeep while the fishermen on shore stared after them. Dr. Uhl said:

"You think a lot of Colonel Calder, General. Perhaps a little more than most commanding officers."

McIntosh stared straight ahead. "He's a valuable man. We need more like him."

"I didn't quite mean that."

"What did you mean?"

"Nothing," Dr. Uhl smiled.

"I have a son myself, General. He's only eleven, but he has dreams too."

McIntosh looked thoughtful. "It's not that simple, Doctor. About my feelings towards Calder. I can't explain it myself. But you know—sometimes I *am* Calder."

Dr. Uhl looked at him, and his face was understanding.

A few minutes later, the jeep was pulling up in front of the

Commune di Gerra, and the tall figure of the Colonel was stepping forward with a crisp salute.

General McIntosh returned it hastily, eager to grasp the Colonel's saluting hand in congratulations.

"You made it," he said, his voice choked. "You made it, Bob. The first man in history? How does it feel?"

"Fine, General McIntosh." Calder grimaced. "In a way . . ."

"I know what you're thinking. You're thinking of the crew. It's tragic that they died just in the moment of their glory. But still, the ship was brought home, Bob. The world won't forget that—"

Dr. Uhl put out his hand and grinned. "It was a great job, Bob. A really great job."

"Look," the General said. "Is there someplace private where we can talk?"

"My office is yours," the Commissario said graciously. "This way gentlemen."

"Good. We've got a lot to talk about, Bob. I want to hear everything—every single minute of it." He gripped Calder's arm and led him into the building.

On a mountainous highway not many miles from the Commune di Gerra, the truck and trailer of Dr. Leonardo moved cautiously over the narrow road.

Night was falling slowly, the sun descending in a spectacular splash of color into the Mediterranean.

On the seat beside the old man, Marisa dozed.

A wind came up from the south, and Dr. Leonardo pulled his collar around his throat.

In the rear of the truck, the wind caught the loose edge of the tarpaulin, and it flapped in uneven rhythm against the cage inside.

But the flapping didn't disturb the cage's occupant.

The cage was empty.

The Alfa Romeo, long and shining, it's black body like mirrors in the night, drew up before the Commune di Gerra, its official flags fluttering from the front fenders. The villagers who were still lingering outside gaped at the magnificence of this vehicle. Never had such a splendid automobile stopped in the village of Gerra, and with such a distinguished passenger.

When the elderly gentleman, with his fine white hair and mustachios, stepped forth from the car, a murmur of awe came from the onlookers. They did not know this Signore Contino by name, but they could tell from his stance, his carriage, his clothing, his automobile, that he was a government official of dignity and importance.

The Commissario's Carbinieri saluted as the new arrival came to the entrance of the building. They escorted him within, past the ospedale, directly to the headquarters of the Police.

It was a bare, shabby office, and unimpressive stage for such an impressive man as the Commissario to perform upon. But the presence of Signore Contino gave it suddenly an air of prestige. The Commissario rose from behind his battered desk as the Carbineri announced the name of the visitor from Rome.

"Avante, per favore," the police chief said.

"Grazie," Contino replied, with a slight bow.

"I am honored." The Commissario turned to the others. "Gentlemen, may I present Signore Contino of the Italian Department of State. The General McIntosh, Dr. Judson Uhl, Colonel Calder."

Contino nodded to each man in turn.

The General cleared his throat.

"I thank you, Signore, for coming so promptly. And I thank your Government for expressing its desire to cooperate in this matter. I must beg you however, for the moment to observe complete secrecy.

"It is understood," Contino said.

McIntosh rubbed his chin and leaned against the edge of the desk. He folded his arms, his face grave.

"What I have to say to you will sound incredible. But I assure you that it is true."

He paused and looked at the Colonel.

"Colonel Calder here has just returned from an expedition to Venus."

The old man cocked his head, as if uncertain of his own hearing.

"Eh? To, er, Venice? You mean perhaps Venetzia?"

"To *Venus*, Signore, McIntosh said grimly. "The planet Venus."

Contino looked around him, his eyes wary, and then he looked plainly suspicious.

"To the planet Venus?" he repeated.

"That is correct."

The State Department official flapped his arms in the air, and they landed with a thud against his side.

"I had been informed that this matter was connected with something vast. But—the planet Venus!" He turned his eyes on Calder, looking him over as if the Colonel were an alien creature himself.

"Man's first interplanetary voyage," McIntosh said, his own words awing him. "On the return trip, the spaceship was crippled by a meteor. Except for Colonel Calder, the entire crew perished."

"I am grieved," Contino said quietly.

"Now we are faced with a problem," the General continued. "A problem of enormous consequence. In order for you to help us, Signore, I must explain carefully."

The old man sought a chair, and lowered himself without once removing his eyes from the General's face.

"The problem is this. The atmosphere on Venus is such that a human being cannot breathe it and survive. There is carbon dioxide in the air, but no oxygen. We believed that we could develop artificial respiratory equipment that would sustain human life, for a limited time, on this planet. We created such equipment and after the first successful landing was made, it operated satisfactorily for some time. But it wasn't fool-proof. There were elements in the air, dust-clouds of some extraordinary nature, that suddenly poisoned our men. Several members of our expedition died there before the others realized the danger. Dr. Sharman, the chief scientist aboard, also became fatally ill. He died here after the ship's crash."

Contino's face was a study in wonder.

"Fascinating!" he said. "Horrible—but fascinating!"

"But this is the important part, Signore Contino. On that ship was a particular sealed metal container—" The General measured the air with his hands. It was approximately this long, and this diameter. In it, Colonel Calder informs me, is an unborn specimen of life on this planet. Of animal life, Doctor?"

Dr. Uhl flipped the pages of Dr. Sharman's notebook."Sharman wrote that he considered it so," the scientist replied. "Or very nearly so."

"Thank you."

The General unfolded his arms, and his hands grasped the edge of the desk tightly.

"It is of the greatest importance that we recover that sealed container. We must discover what physiological way of life is able to survive and flourish on Venus. Not until that secret has been learned can another expedition expect to return. With such a secret, we believe we can develop breathing equipment that will work effectively, permit man to explore this planet without danger of poisoning, and bring back the wealth that lies buried there. Yes, I said wealth, Sognore. For in the few days that Colonel Calder and his crew were able to survive on the planet, the confirmed what the astronomical predictions stated. They discovered rare and precious minerals that would be of vast benefit to the security and the progress of our civilization. We must return. We *have* to return! Get back!"

Contino bowed.

"I am at your service, General McIntosh. In what way may I assist?"

"We shall need divers first of all, divers to descend to the wreck of the space vessel and search for the specimen."

The government official went briskly to the telephone.

"They shall be here before morning."

The greatest gunfighter in the West put away his wooden pistol, his interest in Indians and rustlers suddenly abated. There was a new, excitement for his young eyes, in the throng that was gathering at the foot of the wharf of Gerra.

Pepe edged closer to see what current wonders were on display. When he saw what was happening, his mouth dropped open, and he squealed involuntarily with excitement. This was a week of weeks! There were divers climbing into boats, strong muscled men with big pipes strapped to their broad backs, and round windows of glass dangling from straps around their necks. They carried odd rubbery things in their hand, that flapped like the fins of great sea-monsters.

When he was closer still, he could hear the voices of the men on the shore, as they spoke to the divers before they rowed away.

"Buona fortuna! one of them cried, and Pepe recognized the man in the uniform with the birds on the shoulders, the man who had lain stricken and unconscious on the stretcher only two days before.

"Grazie," the divers replied, and they pulled on the oars away from the beach.

Then a large, impressive gentleman was speaking, a man also of the uniform americano, with even more decorations on his chest, and silver stars shining on his shoulders. Pepe regarded this hero with respect.

"And now, Signore Commissario," the General was saying, "if it is possible, I would like to speak to the fishermen who went aboard the wreck."

"But of course," the Commissario said. "They are waiting for you."

"Me! Me!" Pepe thought. "I too, was with Verrico's fishing boat! But he was too frightened of the impressive man with the stars to come forward. What if they wished him to return Dr. Leonardo's two hundred lira?

"Verrico!" the Commissario was calling. "Mondello! A moment of your time, please."

Pepe walked nearer as his fishing companions responded. If Verrico did not fear, why should he?"

"Si, Signore Commissario?" Verrico said.

"General, this is Verrico and this is Mondello. They are the two men who went into the great ship before she sank, and brought forth Colonel Calder and the other man." He looked at the fishermen. "The American General wishes to speak of an item of great value."

"Si, Signore," Mondello said eagerly. "We will tell you what we know."

"First, let me congratulate and thank you for your heroic work in the ship," the General said. "Your actions have been recorded and sent to the capitols of your country and mine, and I wouldn't be surprised if both Governments award you men citations of bravery."

Verrico looked flustered, but Mondello's chest swelled proudly.

"However, a far more urgent matter concerns us now," the Gen-

Slowly, the beast came out of shock.

eral continued. "We are looking for something that was brought in the aircraft. It is a metal cylinder about this high and this round." He pointed towards the diver's boat, now well out at sea. "Very probably, it went down with the ship, somewhere out there. But there's always the possibility that it was knocked loose and will drift ashore somewhere. Today, tomorrow—who can tell!"

Pepe was startled at his words. A cylinder, like the one he had found! Would he be published for selling it? Or was there perhaps a greater reward for him in revealing his information. His mind was torn between fright, avarice, and awe.

"It's important that we recover that cylinder," the General said. "So important that we find the cylinder and its contents that I have offered a reward of a half million lira to anyone who discovers it. Please have that information spread around among your people."

Pepe could contain himself no longer. A half million lira! He could buy a thousand cowboy hats! A horse! Boots! A silver saddle! Why, perhaps he could buy Taixas itself!

"Signore—"

The General looked at him curiously.

"Signore, you will not take my hat from me?" He smiled.

"Silencio!" Verrico growled. "The American General is speaking to us, little one."

"But Signore—"

Colonel Calder saw something in the boy's face. He said: "Wait, this may be something. What is it, son? What is it you wish to say?"

"It—it is only if I speak about this thing from the ship, you must promise me that I may keep my—my hat from the great country of Taixas."

They were all looking at Pepe now. Calder dropped to one knee to put his face close to the boy's.

"Of course you may keep your hat. But what do you know of the big container?"

Pepe eyed him shrewdly. "And there is the matter of a half million lira. How much is that."

"A lot of money."

"Sufficient to purchase for me a cowboy horse like they ride in Taixas?"

"Enough to buy many horses." Calder's mouth was dry. The anger was coming on him, but he knew he must be gentle with the boy. "What do you know about the container?"

"You promise me about the hat—and the horses?"

McIntosh said: "You have our promise, son."

Pepe's face glowed. "It is there!"

He ran quickly towards a rocky cave diagonally across the beach. They followed after him, and saw him point proudly to the hidden cylinder.

"And now," may I have my horses, per favore?"

Colonel Calder grabbed for the cylinder, peered inside and thew it away in disgust.

"Empty!"

His arm went out and grabbed the boy's shoulder roughly. He started to shake him and the General had to command him to stop.

"Easy, Bob," the General said. "That's not the way."

"But I know where it is!" Pepe sobbed. "The thing that was inside!"

"Where? Where?"

"I took it to the Professor Leonardo, I sold it to him for two hundred lira—" He took off his Stetson. "That is how I have the hat from Taixas.

"This Professor Leonardo," the General said, turning to the fishermen. "Where is he?"

Verrico shrugged. "He must be somewhere on the road to Messina by now. He said he must go to Roma."

Calder put his arm on the big man's wrist, holding it harder than necessary. Verrico suffered the indignity in silence without complaint.

"How will we find him?" the Colonel said. "How will we know him?"

"You will know him easily my friend. He drives a truck with a house that follow it like a goat."

"A trailer!"

"Find it as quickly as you can," the General said urgently. "I'll wait for the divers."

"Yes, sir!"

"Commissario, if you and your men will accompany the Colonel—"

"But certainly!" the officer bowed.

"Besides," McIntosh grinned. I have to see a man about a horse—and a half million lira."

He tousled Pepe's hair, and the boy sighed with gratitude for the blessing that had rained upon him from the Sicilian heavens. He had really struck it rich.

It had been a long, hard drive, made more difficult by the steep mountainous highway. There was treachery in it, too, for there had been rain in the mountains the previous evening.

Marisa, spelling her grandfather at the wheel, drove slowly down the winding road, her eyes peering into the darkness.

But there was more on the girl's mind than the dangers of the ride. The events of the past hours had suddenly brought the past into her mind. The sight of men in uniform, the talk of stricken aircraft, the wounds of the men in the hospital—these things brought sharp and painful images of the war years to her mind.

She tried to blacken out the scenes that paraded before her inner eye: the cruel fences of the concentration camp outside Rome. The sounds of bombing, and the shrieks of men and women caught beneath the descending fire. And then, cruelest image of all, she saw her mother's face and heard her gentle voice; felt her father's touch on her cheeks, and remembered how good his whiskered cheek had felt against hers. Then she remembered the day of the bombardment of Naples, and the moment she came running towards the heap of rubble that had once been home . . .

She shook her head at nothing, and tried to think of her life in America. America, where everything was so different, and so calm. Where there was so little fear of war past and war future . . .

And yet, the American Colonel, with his rude manners and bitter voice—was it war that guided his inexplicable actions. Was it some kind of war game being played at their doorstep?

The wind cut sharply through the cab of the truck, and Marisa said:

"Such wind! Can you hear it, grandfather?"

"Yes. There is a sound somewhere in the truck—from the rear—"

They listened together, and heard the rhythmic flapping of the loose tarpaulin.

"Stop for a moment, mi cara. The canvas has come loose."

She put her foot on the brake, and brought the vehicle to a stop. Her grandfather emerged first, and she followed, stretching her stiff muscles and yawning.

"Such a relief . . ." she said, and walked around to the rear of the truck. Her grandfather was tugging at the ropes that held the canvas. She went to his side to help.

"It has occurred to me," Dr. Leonardo said, as if continuing a conversation that had never begun, "that our strange friend is perhaps a mutation. But of what species? This I cannot say. And there is always the possibility that it might be a throwback to a prehistoric and unclassified—"

Marisa scream cut into his speech.

"What is it?" the Doctor said.

She screamed again, and he saw the three-taloned claw wrapped about her slim wrist. She jerked her arm away, and the grip was broken.

Yet still Marisa screamed rubbing her wrist in horror and backing away from the truck.

"Grandfather! Grandfather!"

The tarpaulin, constructed of strong canvas, and made even stronger by the dampness of the night, was being split apart before their eyes—rended easily as if its composition were mere tissue. The hole gaped wide, and the thing that was ripping its way through to freedom hissed in a terrible sibilant sound that sent Dr. Leonardo and his grandchild staggering away in terror.

"How big . . . how big . . ." the Doctor muttered.

Gone was the three-foot creature that had been a prisoner in the zoologist's cage. The cage itself had been twisted out of shape, its metal bars torn and broken as if they had been threads of cotton. The beast loomed up in the rear of the truck fully the size of a man, twice as large as before, twice as horrifying.

Then it leaped!

Marisa's shriek rebounded over the mountaintops, and her grandfather croaked helplessly and reached for her arm. The beast landed on its feet before them, waving its three-taloned claws, menacingly in the air, the sounds erupting from its throat filled with alien terror. They backed away, slowly, clinging to each other.

"Don't move, my child," Dr. Leonardo whispered. "It doesn't intend us harm . . .it won't hurt us . . ."

"Oh, God! Marisa said. "The size of the thing—so soon—so soon—"

The beast remained frozen in its frightening attitude, as if uncertain of its next maneuver.

Then, a terrifying thing, it started at them.

"No!" Dr. Leonardo cried as the creature rushed towards them. He pushed his granddaughter aside, out of its path.

But the creature wasn't bent on attack. It brushed by them, its ugly eyes fixed on some unguessable destination.

Then it was gone.

They stared after it, their breaths rapid.

Are you hurt?" the Doctor said.

"No," Marisa gasped. "No, I don't think so. Maybe—maybe I frightened it as much as it frightened me. Its claw—"

"What about it?"

"It was strangely hot—"

She looked at her wrist, in curiosity and revulsion.

"Listen!" the Doctor said.

They cocked their ears into the night, and the shrill scream of sirens broke the silence.

"Someone's coming," Marisa said. "Thank God—"

There were two jeeps approaching, and as they came in view of the truck and trailer, they braked sharply to a halt. At first, Dr.

Leonardo and the girl were alarmed at the number of strange men who jumped out. There were armed Carbinieri, the Commissario of the Gerra police force, an unfamiliar balding gentleman in civilian clothes and—

Marisa saw the man in the uniform, and recognized her own bandages on his arm and forehead. The sight of him somehow caused her to become more confident and composed.

"I beg your pardon," he said to her grandfather. "But you must be Professor—"

Dr. Leonardo wouldn't wait for the formalities. He turned to the Commissario and said: "There is a strange animal, Signore. We were carrying it in our truck, and it broke away—"

"Wait!" A strange animal—like nothing you've ever seen before?"

"Like something *no* one has seen before," the Doctor said emphatically. "I had been keeping it in a cage in back of the truck, but it broke out. I do not know where such strength comes from. It grabbed my granddaughter, and then ran off—"

The Colonel looked at the girl for the first time.

"Hello! It's you—almost-a-doctor."

His words brought her chin into the air, and she turned her head aside. But instead of noticing her haughty gesture, he continued to speak to Dr. Leonardo.

"Tell me about the creature, Professor. It's all right—I'm Colonel Robert Calder, United States Air Force. The—the creature is connected with an important mission."

"And I," Dr. Leonardo said proudly, "am not Professor Leonardo, My title, sir, is Doctor. Doctor of zoology. This is my granddaughter, Marisa."

Marisa looked at Colonel Calder, but his worried face didn't respond to her glance. She didn't like being ignored, but the hard-eyed young Colonel was intent upon learning more about the escaped beast.

"The creature," he said impatiently. "You must tell me everything you know. Everything, mind."

"First it was this high," Dr. Leonardo said, measuring with

tremulous hands. "Then this height. And now it is tall, nearly as tall as a man. Bigger—bigger."

Dr. Uhl spoke. "Is that the normal rate of growth?"

"Not as far as I know," Calder said. "The only data we have are in Dr. Sharman's notes." He frowned at the old man. "And where is the animal now?"

"It fled into the woods. It has amazing strength, Colonel; the very bars of its cage were torn apart. It's dangerous—"

"Let's go," Calder said. But Dr. Leonardo stopped his departure.

"Please! You must tell me. I must know! What is that creature? Where does it come from?"

"I can't answer questions now. Best thing for you and your granddaughter now, Doctor, is to keep heading towards Rome, away from here."

"Let us go with you!"

"Sorry, Doctor. Not now. But thanks for all your help.

He turned and gestured towards the others.

"Into the woods," he said.

"We'll have to track the beast down on foot!"

They moved on towards the wooded area. Marisa looked after them, particularly at the retreating back of the rude and single-minded young officer.

"It looks like my patient's recovered," she said ruefully. But his manners are no better."

"Come Marisa." Dr. Leonardo headed back for the truck. "We must make Rome by dawn. There are many things I must tell them at the Museo . . ."

CHAPTER VI

Horror Takes Shape

THE creature hungered.

The hunger was sharp in its vitals. Unsatisfied juices oozed into its mouth. It's three-taloned hands quivered with its need. Its eyes burned with the desire for nourishment.

It staggered through the thick underbrush, a blind instinct taking control of its strangely articulated legs, driving it forward to some unknown source of food. A food it had never tasted, but a food that millennia of inbreeding on a world far away had mad necessary for its survival.

The food wasn't here. It waited somewhere beyond this tangled wilderness, and the creature was determined to reach it.

A whinnying sound halted its progress. Four-legged beasts, with long silky manes and narrow shanks, became frightened at its approach. They bolted from beneath the large tree where they had been grazing peacefully, their manes streaming out behind them.

The creature regarded their flight blankly, and moved forward again.

Then he saw the structures.

They were small, snug buildings that housed the excitable two-legged things which had placed him in a metal prison and brought him high to the mountains. There was a fence that enclosed more of the silky-maned four-legged beasts, and they too whinnied as he came into view.

From further off, a bleating noise was heard.

The creature joined the night-chorus of sounds. His breathing became heavy. He grunted and hissed in defiance and hatred of the world that was now his home, his tail swishing back and forth on the tall grass. Then he roared a challenge eons old to the universe at large, and lumbered towards the sound of bleating animals in the field.

They were smaller animals than he had surprised under the tree, animals covered with kinky hair. Their bleating intensified as he came upon them, and then they broke and scattered in instinctive fear of the alien creature.

But one didn't flee. A small animal, to small for wisdom, tugged at the resisting grass with his tiny mouth. A rumble came from the deep throat of the creature as he moved towards it.

Then he stopped.

His dragon's head raised in the air, as if sensing something more important than this innocent target of his wrath. An implanted desire stirred within him, and he turned from the tiny animal and headed back towards the structures of the two-legged ones.

Vittorio grumbled at the pain in his back.

Each day, the soil of the farmland seemed to resist his efforts more and more. Today, his plow had struck a buried rock in the fields, and the blades, never to sharp for the unyielding ground, were now hopelessly in need of repair.

It had been a good life once, when he was young and strong and Maria was alive, and the stubbornness of the soil had seemed only a rightful challenge. But now he was old, and alone, and his back hurt.

In the barnyard, the mongrel dog he had taken for companionship, began to bark. The sound was an annoying yap, and he shouted:

"Silencio, Carlo!"

Still Carlo barked, and Vittorio muttered imprecations on the animal's shaggy head. If he wasn't so tired, he would have thrashed the beast into quiet. Not to hard, of course; just enough to silence him for the night. It was no use hurting your only friend.

Then he heard the squawking of the chickens in the hen house, and he shook his head in chagrin. That was the way of animals; one complained and the others must join the chorus. Perhaps they were not so different from people.

But when Vittorio heard the whinnying of the horses in the barn, he became curious.

He went to the window and peered through it. For a moment, he thought he saw a shadow cross the path of moonlight in the barnyard, a shadow bigger than a marauding fox.

He pulled on his boots, groaning at the effort, and then lifted his rusty shotgun from the wall. He took the coal oil lantern from the table, and went out into the night.

The creature walked into the building, its walls hung with strange objects of hide and wood and metal. There were piles of stuff like dried grass everywhere, and in the rear, two enclosures held more of the four-legged whinnying beasts it had encountered in the meadow. They too became over-wrought at his presence, throwing themselves against the wooden pens in fright. Their neighing was hysterical; their hooves thundered against the stalls.

Then one of the horses broke from its prison, and went streaming out of the building. The others soon followed him, and the creature stood back and regarded their flight in puzzlement.

He moved further into the barn, and found sacks filled with peculiar grains. He ripped them open and overturned them, sniffing the contents and turning away with a hiss of discontent.

Then a sack yielded a powdery substance. He scooped some into his three-taloned hands and put it to his mouth. He growled with pleasure at the taste, at the warmth it imparted to his complaining stomach. Contentedly, the creature dined on the yellowish powder from the farmer's stores.

But his meal wasn't to be peaceful.

A yapping, snarling, glowering animal was standing menacingly in the doorway, a small belligerent thing with fiery eyes and ridiculous short legs. It hesitated only for a moment, and then sprung to engage the creature in combat.

At first, the suddenness of the attack caught the creature off balance. Then it met the challenge with a roar of hatred.

The dog's teeth tried to sink their way into the scaly throat of the thing from Venus; its claws raked the tough hide viciously. But the sharp talons and unworldly strength of the creature soon took command. Broken and bleeding, the animal was torn from its grip and flung disdainfully in a corner of the building.

Vittorio came into the barn, just as the awful sounds of the death-struggle were fading away. He held his coal oil lantern high to shed a pool of light around his feet.

"Carlo!" he called. "Carlo!"

The dog didn't respond. It was strange; he had never failed to heed Vittorio's voice before. He went to the barn.

"Hey, Carlo! What's all the noise, eh, boy? What you got there, eh? You catch yourself a nice big rat, Carlo? Carlo!"

He stepped inside, and the lantern's gleam fell upon the animal's mutilated body.

The farmer stared at it in horror and disbelief, still not feeling a sense of loss, not willing to recognize that Carlo, faithful Carlo was dead.

"Carlo," he whispered. "I did not mean that, about the beating. That was an old man's talk . . ."

He was about to touch the body, when a sound in the loft drew his frightened attention.

The sight of the awesome, dragon's head above him froze his features in terror.

"Don't move," a voice said behind him. "Back out very slowly."

Vittorio's old body couldn't obey the command. He continued to stare at the monstrous creature that had come to roost in the straw of his loft, his eyes running with tears of grief for his lost friend, his heart pounding in superstitious dread of the monster.

"Easy, old man," Colonel Calder said tightly. "Come away from there. Come out slowly."

Then fingers were touching Vittorio's sleeve, and he finally reacted. He backed away from the frightful sight of the creature's jaws, and then turned to see who had come to his rescue.

"Outside," Calder said. "You, too Dr. Uhl. We have to work this out.

The civilian scientist gaped at his first look at the thing from Venus.

"Incredible!" he said. "Even after you told me, Bob—I could never have believed it—"

"We'll talk about it outside," Calder repeated tensely. He stretched out his arms, his eyes fixed on the thing in the farmer's loft, pushing the men outside the barn.

When they were all out, he shut the door carefully, and turned to the Commissario.

"The creature must be captured alive, Commissario. That is our main task. I saw a wagon outside; perhaps your men could bring it into the barn."

The police chief waved to his men. "Il carreto! Pronto!"

"And we'll need a pole, a sharp wooden pole."

"Una pala—subito!"

Dr. Uhl went to the door of the barn, his expression awed. I've had nightmares in my time," he said. "But never anything like this. Were there many such creatures on Venus, Bob?"

"Hundreds, perhaps thousands. It's hard to say, Dr. Uhl; we had so little time to explore the planet. But from what we saw of them, we figured that they're really not ferocious—only when provoked. It's my guess that the poor dog attacked first."

"Perhaps Venus is going through its prehistoric period now, just as Earth had to. The only resemblance I can find is to a tyrannosaurus, or some such beast. Could that be the answer?"

"Maybe so," Calder said. "And who can say what they'll evolve eventually? Maybe something better than Man, something that won't be terrified of anything just because of its ugliness . . ."

Behind them, the Commissario was urging on his Carbinieri, who were pushing the farmer's hay wagon towards the barn door. They backed it up to the doorway, steering the ancient vehicle by its wagon tongue.

"Good," Calder said. He grasped the side of the wagon and shook it. "Not the sturdiest cage in the world for our friend, but I suppose it will have to do."

"Signore—"

It was the old farmer, a long sharp-pointed wooden pole in his hand.

"Grazie," Calder said.

"Signore, the dog, Carlo—"

"Yes?"

The old man bowed his head. "Nothing . . . I am saddened. The dog, it was only a mongrel, and it was lazy, not good for much. But Carlo was my friend, Signore. This thing in the barn. What will be the end of all this?"

"You won't have to worry about it," Calder said crisply, taking the pole from his hands. "Exactly what I need. I'm going to try to prod the creature into the wagon. If I succeed, get ready to slam the tailgate closed."

Dr. Uhl said: "Can I help."

"No, just slam the gate in time." His face hardened. "I have to capture it alive," he said flatly. "Alive and unhurt, Commissario." He pointed to the police chief's gun. "That means no shooting. Understand?"

The Commissario nodded grimly, and wiped his face with his palm.

They opened the door, and cleared a path for the Colonel to enter the barn. He held the pole lightly beneath his arm, like a lancer going into battle, and walked slowly into the darkness.

The Carbinieri rolled the wagon in after him, and the men gathered at its side to watch the battle joined.

There was moonlight on the floor of the barn, and its beams

cast an unearthly light on the scaly hide of the creature hiding in the loft. It was making ugly, warning noises in its throat.

Calder reached out and prodded him slightly. A three-taloned hand slapped out, and the Colonel retreated quickly. Then he shoved the pole forward again, and once more the creature flailed at it.

"I don't want to hurt you," Calder muttered. "If you could only understand . . ."

He raised the pole again.

The creature leaped!

Calder backed away hastily, stumbled on some slippery substance on the floor of the barn, He recovered just in time to keep the pole between the infuriated thing from Venus and himself.

It stood rigid, its eyes gleaming in the moonlight, its jaws parted and moist with bitterness and anger.

It moved swiftly to the right and to the left, its claws raking out in an effort to grasp the tantalizing pole. It couldn't stop its rapid movement, couldn't stop its elusive jabs at its body.

"Easy, easy," Calder muttered, trying to force the beast towards the wagon.

The sounds in the creature's throat were now awful to hear. The pole taunted it, and it could do nothing. It roared and grumbled, and slashed out helplessly. But slowly, the pole was pushing it backwards, back to the entrance of the building where the wooden prison awaited the beast.

The Commissario, Dr. Uhl, and the others crowded closer to the scene of the battle, sensing that the moment of capture had almost come. Dr. Uhl's face was a portrait of strain and tension; the Commissario, a man more used to violent deeds, merely looked worried.

Again Calder prodded the creature towards the open gate of the wagon.

"Now!" Calder shouted.

Dr. Uhl sprang forward to ready the gate, to slam it shut before the creature could bolt away. But his action came a second too late; the creature lunged in the direction of the spectators.

Vittorio the old farmer, flung his hands up in fear, and his lantern slipped from his fingers.

"Look out! Calder dried.

Vittorio, crazed with fright, threw himself towards the wall of the barn. His fingers closed around the handle of a pitchfork, and he waved it in defense. The creature came after him, and Calder cursed at the farmer's interference.

"Put that thing down!" he barked. "We're doing alright—it's just a matter of—"

The distraction was all that the beast from Venus needed. With a swoop of its strong right arm, it swept the pole out of the Colonel's hand and turned to flee. A Carbinieri raised his rifle, and Calder tore it from his grasp.

"No shooting! I said no shooting!"

But the rifle wasn't the only weapon Calder had to fear. Vittorio, the old farmer, hate and loathing in his eyes, was raising the pitchfork high above his head, and with a shrill cry, he drove it deep into the back of the creature.

"No!" Calder cried, his voice almost a wail.

The creature emitted a yell of torment, a cry of the damned. He shook his scaly body until the piercing tines of the fork were loosened, and the implement thudded to the floor of the barn.

The his taloned hands reached out in rage and grasped Vittorio. Its powerful arms closed around the old farmer, and they rolled together to the ground.

Calder jumped to the wall and grabbed a shovel, heading to help the old man. His screams were frightful; the creature was mauling Vittorio as mercilessly as he had destroyed Carlo, the dog.

Calder raised the shovel over his head, and beat at the scaly figure with all the strength in his arms. Nothing seemed to injure it, but the attack diverted the creature enough to cause him to release his death-grip on the old man's throat. He snarled and whirled upon Calder. The Colonel raised the shovel again, and the creature lashed out.

Calder fell; the bandage on his arm reddened with blood once more.

The Commissario had his gun drawn. Calder looked up at him helplessly, ready to shake his head no again. But then the creature turned once more to the mutilated old man on the floor, and the Commissario fired.

It was the signal for general action by the Carbinieri. They pulled

Calder away from the danger zone, and began pumping bullet's in the creature's direction. Firing, they backed out towards the entrance of the barn.

The Commissario swore loudly. "He is the devil himself! Bullets have no effect! He cannot be killed—"

The creature left the old man and snarled defiantly at the men and their weapons. Calder had a gun in his hand now, too, and he fired point-blank at the scaly beast, more to experimentation than anger.

"Outside!" he shouted. "Try and lock him in the barn!"

They reached the entrance and slammed the barn doors closed just as the creature was upon them. They could hear its talons ripping at the wood.

"It's impossible!" Dr. Uhl said shakily. "Bullet's can kill the thing, Bob! Maybe nothing can! That poor old man . . ."

"Hold the doors!" the Commissario shouted to his officers. "Bolt it!"

The doors of the barn creaked and bulged with the creature's efforts to escape. The Carbinieri pushed against it with all their combined strength, but the beast inside seemed to equal it.

Then suddenly, there was no pressure.

"What happened?" Dr. Uhl said.

Calder grimaced. "I don't know. Maybe our friend's given up."

The loud crashing of timber around the other side told a different story.

"Around the side!" Calder yelled.

They went at a trot to the other side of the barn, in the direction of the splintering sound.

"Damn!" Colonel Calder said.

The hole torn in the rotted wood was big enough to permit the escape of a creature twice the size of the beast from the far-off planet of Venus.

They stood around Dr. Leonardo's trailer, watching the Commissario pace nervously back and forth, their faces weary and resigned.

Finally, the police chief halted his march, and turned to Colonel Calder.

"I do not like this thing," he said flatly. "I do not like it!"

"I don't like it much myself, Commissario," The Colonel drawled. "But I don't think we have any choice in the matter. We have to hunt the creature down, no matter how long it takes."

Marisa appeared at the door of the trailer. She came forward to the Colonel's side, but he ignored her.

"Colonel!"

"Yes?"

She looked at Calder and clucked her tongue as if he were a disobedient child.

"I hate to intrude on your precious private thoughts. But I'd *like* to change the bandages on your arm."

He looked down at it, as if seeing the freshly-opened wound for the first time.

"I guess you're right."

"Thanks for the compliment. Come inside the trailer; I have bandages and tape.

He followed her with some reluctance, his head turning in the direction of the escaped creature. Once inside, he sat wearily at the table as the girl went to work with efficient fingers, cutting away the soiled bandage with a scissors.

Her annoyance faded as she wound the fresh cloth around his arm. Her expression became contrite.

"You're worried about what happened—about where the creature's gone."

"We'll find him," Calder said. "We've got to."

"I feel partly responsible for the whole thing. If we knew what we had our hands on, we would have taken greater precautions. But grandfather always takes the academic approach to things—"

"It's not your fault, or Dr. Leonardo's. You couldn't have known what the creature was. Even I wouldn't have guessed that it could grow so rapidly." He sighed in chagrin and exhaustion.

"I guess I haven't been very considerate," Marisa said. "I know you've got a lot on your mind; I shouldn't have expected you to overly polite."

His face softened.

"If that's an apology, I think it went in the wrong direction. All you've done is try to help, and all I've done is snarl at you. That's one of my problems, bullheadedness, temper, whatever you call it. I got the official opinion on that from Uncle Sam."

"I don't understand it."

"Skip it." He smiled and touched her hand. "But when all this is over, maybe you'll let me make a formal apology. Over a table for two in a dark cafe—"

She smiled. "With a candle burning on the table?"

And a bottle of wine . . ."

She put her tools back in the bag, thoughtfully.

"Is it true, what I heard them say? About this creature? Is it true that you found it on—Venus?"

"It's true, all right."

"Venus!" Her eyes glowed. So far away. . . ."

"More than twenty million miles," Calder said. "But now I'm beginning to feel that twenty million Miles isn't really so far. When we go back—"

"Go back? Marisa gasped. "You don't mean that?"

"Of course I mean it. We must go back, or the whole trip was for nothing. All those lives, for nothing. Oh, I don't mean just for the minerals and precious metal—they have importance, sure. But just to do it. Just to make the journey!"

"But why? Why? What makes it so important to you?"

"I don't know," Calder said. "It was like a preview of Hell up there. Great dust clouds, hot orange sky, mist, burning desert. And then that poison in the air, the choking, the pain in the lungs—"

"How terrible!"

"Terrible and wonderful!" Calder said, "I'd never experienced such pain or such fear in my life, Marisa. But I'd go again, if they asked me. And I'd go to Mars—to Neptune—to Jupiter—to the stars!"

She was shaking her head sadly.

"I don't think much of your dream, Colonel. It's like a crazy thirst that can't be quenched. What can such trips bring you? More death? More creatures like that—"

"It makes no difference!"

"It does! she said angrily. "With such an imperfect world here—what gives us the right to seek others? What can we bring them?"

"You don't understand—"

"I do! You men have given up on this world of ours. That's why you look up at space and have your crazy dreams! You don't know how to live on Earth. You kill each other, torture, betray—" Her voice was shrill. "So you want escape, Colonel. That's the real truth, isn't it? Escape from yourselves!"

Surprisingly, there were tears in her eyes.

"Marisa!"

"Oh, let me alone! Go out and kill your poor beast. Show it how well we behave on our planet. Shoot it with your guns—destroy it with your bombs—"

"Hey, hey," he said gently, his arms closing around her comfortingly. "Take it easy, almost-a-doctor. Why so upset?"

She put her head against his shoulder.

"Listen," Calder told her, I'm the last guy in the world that wants to kill the poor thing. It was harmless on its own world. I want to keep it alive, so we can find out how it breathes—how it can survive on Venus when we can't."

She dried her eyes, and moved away from him.

"Your humanity is touching—"

"Whose being bitter now?"

"I'm sorry." She looked up and smiled wanly. "This—this is very unprofessional behavior."

He laughed, and put his arms towards her again.

"Bob!"

They looked towards the door. Dr. Uhl was in the doorway, his face flushed, his hand clutching the notebook they had taken from the dead hands of Dr. Sharman. Marisa's grandfather was behind him, his face reflecting the scientist's excitement.

"What is it?" Calder said.

"Something I found in Sharman's notebook. He wrote that the basic diet of the creatures is sulfur—raw sulphur!"

"Yes, I remember reading that. But what's the point?"

Dr. Leonard stepped forward. "There are rich sulfur beds in Sicily. Not many kilometers from here—"

Panic flared. Would the chains hold?

"From here?"

"Yes! At the base of Mount Etna!"

Calder's fist struck his palm with enthusiasm. "Of course! We'll scour that mountain area in the morning! If the creature's there— we'll capture him!"

Dr. Leonardo spoke to Dr. Uhl. "At that time, Doctor, I would consider it an honor to extend the facilities of the Gardino Zoologica in Roma for its observation and examination."

"Thank you, Dr. Leonardo."

A new voice came from the doorway.

"That will not be necessary gentlemen."

They looked at the stony face of the Commissario of Police.

"There will be no further attempts to capture that monster alive."

"I don't understand," Calder said.

"I must inform you that there is no longer cooperation between us. This monster must be destroyed! It has badly maimed one man—it may kill others. My duty is first to the welfare of my people. A poor second to contribute to such outlandish scientific investigations." He bowed. "I am sorry, gentlemen. But this is how it must be."

He turned to the door again.

"Please Signore Commissario!" Calder said loudly. "Wait a minute! You can't—"

He followed the police chief outside, and saw the Commissario already entering the jeep with three of his Carbinieri. With a grind of its motor, the vehicle started down the road, heading back for Gerra.

The second jeep was quickly occupied by another of the Sicilian policeman, and Calder, his face livid, jumped to stop him from turning the key in the ignition.

"You got a passenger, pal!"

The policeman shook his head violently, and Calder pushed him off the wheel. He staggered out of the door and almost fell to the ground.

"Dr. Uhl!" Calder shouted. The scientist came over at a trot and leaped into the seat beside the Colonel.

"Fermati!" the Carbinieri cried, reaching for his gun as the jeep drove off. "Fermati!" He was frantic with rage.

He lifted the gun in the air but Marisa was behind him. Her arm went out and pulled the weapon down. He looked at her in disgust, and then ruefully put the gun back into the holster.

Dr. Leonardo came to his granddaughter's side.

"Such a violent man," he said softly. "This Colonel Calder. This is a passion with him."

"Yes," Marisa said, staring down the road. "A passion . . ."

CHAPTER VII

Terror Brought to Bay

THERESA slammed the dish of pasta in front of her husband, and Ignacio regarded the eyes stupefied by wine.

"What is the matter? she said shrilly. "Your big stomach has no more room? It has been drowned in Marsala?

"Not hungry," Ignacio muttered. "Give it to the pigs."

"It *is* for the pig. My pig. My big pig Ignacio!"

She put her fists on her wide hips and glowered at him. "Perhaps if you went out and *worked* all day, like all other men, perhaps then you would have some appetite in the evenings!"

He poured himself another red tumblerful of the wine and put the glass to his lips. It was the final straw for Theresa, and Ignacio knew what was to come next. She stomped to the door of their cabin and flung it open.

"Out, pig!" she cried. "Out with the other wild beasts!"

He rose wearily, accustomed to this routine. His legs shuffled across the floor, his hand scratching lazily at his round paunch. At the doorway, he bowed courteously to his wife and mumbled:

"Good night, Signora."

"Good-*bye!*"

She slammed the door after him, and immediately set up a wail inside the cabin, loud enough for him, the pigs, and neighbors a mile away to hear. It failed to change Ignacio's stubbornly vague expression. He yawned, widely and moved off down the road, heading for Louisa's and more wine.

It was a fine, bright night, with a full moon and many stars. He liked looking at the stars, especially when he was carrying wine. They blinked and shifted so merrily under the effects of it. Ah, Marsala was wonderful! He could see *twice* as many stars as the abstainers. Was that not in itself a very good reason for drinking?

Ignacio felt very proud of this clever reasoning, and he began to hum a cheerful song as he trudged down the road towards the village tavern.

But after a while, the long walk began to tire him. He sighed, and sat down on a rock to think things over. The wine felt warm inside him, and he closed his eyes in an invitation to a time of sweet slumber.

The sound that awoke him was a growl.

"Yes, yes Theresa," he said thickly. "I am going now, right now."

Still the growl came, and Ignacio pried open his eyes and looked around him.

"Theresa?" he said.

Then he realized he was in the woods, and that the growl had come from some animal thing. He chuckled to himself, thinking how he would tell the men at Louisa's of his humorous error.

He raised himself from the rock.

The growl became a roar!

Ignacio turned his head swiftly this way and that, until he saw the thing moving among the trees. He rubbed his eyes and tried to erase the image. But the more he rubbed, the more the vision seemed real.

"I see it," he said to himself. But naturally, of course, I do not see it. No one can see such things in Sicily. Therefore, I cannot see it."

The thing in the woods came closer, and its unbelievable head poked from the underbrush and stared at him.

Ignacio's legs began to tremble.

"I do not see it," he said aloud. "I do not see it. But I am afraid it sees *me.*

The thing's jaw parted and the sound that came from its scaly throat made Ignacio shriek in terror. He leaped into the air and turned his back on the creature. Then his leg, which had not moved with such speed since he was a boy, now remembered how to travel. They carried him back up the road, pumping furiously in an over whelming desire to get away from the thing that was not to be seen in Sicily.

He reached the doorway of his cabin in a fifth of the time he had taken to reach the rock in the road. He yanked open the door, shut and bolted it behind him, and stood panting against it with opened mouth and fear-filled saucer eyes.

"What is it? his wife said, pausing at her meal, the pasta still dripping from her fork.

"A beast—a thing—a demon—" Ignacio gasped.

"You are crazy. Crazy with drink!"

"I swear to you! A dragon in Sicily! Fifty feet high! Breathing flames! I saw it with my own eyes!"

She snorted, and continued to eat. "Wine and an empty stomach," she said contemptuously.

Ignacio looked suddenly uncertain.

Then his face became determined. He stalked over to the table and lifted the half-full bottle of Marsala. He took it over to the wash-basin and poured the contents down the drain.

"Never again!" he said forcefully.

Theresa clapped her hands in happiness. "Ignacio—you mean this?"

"Yes! I mean it, Theresa. Never again buy such cheap wine. From now on—only the best!"

General McIntosh scowled at the rude flooring of the Commune di Gerra. Every now and then, the strutting feet of the Commissario of the Gerra Police crossed his line of vision, and his scowl grew broader.

Beside him, the Italian Government official, Signore Contino, watched the Commissario's restless pacing with grave patience.

"This is my position, Signore Contino."

"The safety of the people in this district is *my* affair—my primary affair—as long as I am Commissario." He stopped in front of Contino. "It may be that you will wish me replaced. That, of course, is your privilege. But until then, I intend to function as Commissario."

Signore Contino clucked.

"You are an efficient man, Signore. A man of sincerity. There can be no question of replacing you."

"This Colonel Calder," the Commissario said, his teeth clenched. "Never have I met a man more stubborn. Even when this creature from Hell was tearing at the flesh of an old man before his eyes— he worried for the creature's safety. The *creature's* safety. When our bullets failed to kill the beast, I would swear to the saints that the man was happy. I am not accustomed to such cold-bloodedness, Signore Contino. Even in the days of the *fascisti*—" His face went dark at that memory.

General McIntosh cleared his throat, as if in preamble.

"You're not being wholly fair, Commissario," he said quietly. "I won't try and explain Colonel Calder to you. But you must understand what this man has lived through. You must understand the strange need that drives him. He feels the importance of our explorations in space with all the fervor of a crusade. Maybe he's a fanatic; I don't know myself. But I do know that without that creature from Venus for us to study—alive—the possibilities of future explorations become dim. It was tough enough to make the first voyage. As for the second—with such disastrous results, with so many men dead—public opinion is not going to be on our side. Things are bad and could get worse."

"These are deep problems," Contino said sadly.

"Too deep, perhaps, for me! The Commissario stepped in front of the General. "I must tell you, General, that at daybreak, I intend to use every means at my disposal to hunt down and destroy that creature before it actually kills someone.

"You can't!"

They looked towards the doorway at the man who had spoken. Colonel Calder's face was wrathful as he strode into the room, followed by Dr. Uhl.

"Bob—" the General said.

"He can't do it, General! Not before—"

"Bob!"

"Yes sir?"

"May I remind you that the Commissario is a Sicillian police chief, performing the duties of his office?"

"Yes, sir, but—Calder's face changed as a thought struck him. "Would there be any objection if Dr. Uhl and I tried to track the animal and take it alive?"

"Yes," Dr. Uhl said eagerly. "Before the Commissario has it destroyed—"

McIntosh shrugged. "No objection from me. But from what I've heard of the beast it won't be that easy." He looked at Signore Contino. "What do you think, Signore?"

Contino said: "How do you propose to do this? How will you go about it?"

"I've been thinking about it," Calder said eagerly. "I remembered something we found out about the creatures, by accident. We had set up power lines outside the ship, and one of the beasts got careless and tried to chew them up. They weren't high voltage lines, but the charge was still strong enough to stun the creature into senselessness. That means they[re extremely susceptible to electric shock. Con trolled voltage can paralyze it. If we could get us two helicopters and a squad of armed paratroopers, we might be able to drop an electrically-charged wire net on the beast."

He looked back and forth at the General and Signore Contino. "All I ask is permission to *try.*"

Contino pursed his lips.

"If it can be done—before human life is threatened—then the Italian Government has no objection."

"Thank you, sir!"

McIntosh touched his arm. "You'll have your 'copters first thing in the morning . . ."

The giant whirly bird, its motors roaring and its rotors spinning, pushed itself off the air strip and hung like some peculiar insect about eight feet in the air.

The crew chief, a thick-shouldered Sergeant with a grinning face black with grease, ducked beneath the upraised fuselage and beckoned for his men to follow. They came on the run, dragging a huge net of steel wiring, and began fastening it to the undercarriage of the helicopter. When the job was completed, he commanded them again, and they scattered.

"Up you go! he shouted.

The helicopter's rotors increased their revolutions, and the big craft rose into the air.

Colonel Calder and Dr. Uhl, standing to one side of the air strip, watched in suspense as the pilot reached his arm over the side of the cabin, tugging at the releasing wire. The net was freed of its fastening, and it plummeted to the ground.

"Right on target!" the crew chief grinned.

He came running towards the Colonel as the 'copter descended once more.

The hook's working fine, sir. Maybe we out to try a few more dry runs.

:No," Calder said. "We don't have the time to spare. We'll just have to pray that the net doesn't jam when we're over our target.

"Yeah," the chief grinned. "This here target, sir, I hear it's some kind of big lizard—"

"Something like that. Only a little uglier than any lizard you ever saw, Sergeant. And bigger. It was the height of a man, last time we saw it. It's probably bigger now."

"Sounds like fun. Shoulda brought my camera."

Dr. Uhl smiled at him. "You won't have time for pictures, Sergeant. If that charged net doesn't knock the creature out, we'll all be pretty busy. Bullets don't have any effect on it."

The crew chief's smile became strained. Then he looked over at the soldiers who were loading sacks into the helicopter.

"What's that for, sir?"

"Sulfur," Calder told him. "I'm taking on a load of sulphur to feed our prisoner when we capture it."

Dr. Uhl watched the loading, his face glum.

"Yes. If the Commissario doesn't capture it first."

A signal from the first 'copter caught the attention of the crew chief.

"Looks like we're ready to board 'Copter One, sir."

"Good." Calder looked at the Doctor. "You take the first 'copter, Doc. I'll take the second with the men. And Doc—"

"Yes?"

"That net you're carrying. It'll be like a parachute, Doc—it's got to work the first time."

Dr. Uhl grinned and hurried off.

Calder headed for the second helicopter warming up on the airstrip. A squad of soldiers, carbines strapped to their field packs, were entering the craft. Two of them carried a portable generator. The Colonel hopped in beside the pilot, and waved two fingers at him.

"All aboard. Let's go!"

Even as Colonel Calder's helicopter were readying for the take-off, the Commissario and his Carninieri were already on the track of the beast.

Not since the war had such a grim contingent appeared on the rugged Sicilian countryside. Uniformed, tight-lipped men, heavily armed with pistols, carbines, M-3's. There were flame-throwers, too, with the long ugly snouts and the promise of searing death in their black, ugly muzzles.

The men walked swiftly, heading for a pile of flat rocks ahead, the panting police dogs straining at their leashes by their side.

"Wait," the Commissario said.

He stepped forward to mount the rise and survey the country-side with his binoculars.

Something moved in range of his lenses, and he let the binoculars fall to his chest. Then he gestured the men forward.

His Sergeant-at-arms came alongside. "Did you see him, Commissario? The big beast from the heavens?"

"Don't look so frightened, Enrico. Yes, I have seen the beast. He is big and ugly, but he is not invincible. We must not have any fear of him. With our guns and our flame-throwers—"

Enrico muttered and crossed himself. "They say guns do not harm him."

"Then we will use fire. Fermati!"

He halted the men again, and his arm pointed to the rippling water beneath them.

"There! By the river!"

Their eyes strained to see, and the police dogs began to bay.

"The creature!" Enrico gasped. He tugged at his gunbelt, his face white.

"Wait! We must get closer—"

Now they were in full sight of the beast, rearing on its splayed legs to stare at them in surprise and anger at being disturbed. It was the dogs who were most reckless; they tore their way from the leashes of the Carbinieri, and went running towards the startled monster at the river's edge.

The creature bellowed at the barking animals streaming towards it. Then it turned and made for a high, tree-dotted incline some ten yards away.

"He escapes! Enrico cried.

"No! the Commissario said. "The incline is too steep—he is caught—"

The beast's predicament encouraged them. One after another, the Carbinieri drew their pistols and began to fire at the monster. Desperately, the beast way trying to scale the incline and escape the rapidly - approaching force that was coming to do him hurt.

"We've got him! Enrico cried joyfully.

But even as the words came from his mouth, they saw the creature rear back and make a mighty spring towards the crest of the incline. For a moment, its foot slipped on the loose shale, then its taloned hands dug into the rock and held firm. Another second and it was atop the incline bellowing defiantly at its pursuers.

They stood below and fired at it, without effect on the scaly hide. It hissed and growled, and then turned to vanish behind a rim of rocks.

"After it!" the Commissario yelled. "Don't let it escape!"

They made an assault upon the steep side of the incline. Laboriously, they made the climb, the rocks slipping beneath their feet in miniature landslides. When they came to the top of the talus, the creature turned upon them with a snarl.

The men with the incendiary weapons came hastily to take the front position before the Commissario, planting themselves in firing attitudes directly in front of the threatened creature.

"Fire!"

A whoosh of flame burst from the snouts, aimed directly at the beast. Tips of fire reached it, and the creature screamed in agony and turned to flee.

"After him! After him!"

The flamethrowers were on the chase, fire spewing from their weapons. Again, the scorching white tips touched the creature. Its scream was wild; it made for the safety of a large boulder surrounded by shrubbery. The flames crackled into the dry brush, and it burst into a ball of fire.

"The smoke!" Enrico said, "Be careful!"

White clouds were pouring from the flaming bush, forming a smoke-screen between the Commissario's men and the creature, choking their lungs and blocking their view while the alien beast fled.

"Back! Back!" the Commissario ordered, gathering his forces away from the windward side of the smoke and flames. Angrily, he hefted his binoculars to his eyes and tried to pierce the white fog that his own weapons had created.

But his eyes found nothing.

"We have lost him," he said bitterly. "Now we must separate, so that we can cover more territory. The beast must be found!"

The helicopter dipped low over the terrain, and Colonel Calder peered over the side and pointed down to the billowing smoke.

"Forest fire! he shouted.

"Want to go down?"

"No! But let's drop and have a look—"

The pilot leaned on the stick, and the whirlybird descended at a steep angle in the direction of the fire. They scanned the area for some five minutes, but saw nothing.

Then the Colonel spotted something in the distance. He clapped his hand on the pilot's shoulder to draw his attention.

"Look! I think we've found him!"

"Mother of God! the pilot said, at his first sight of their prey.

In the distance, they saw the creature standing beside a bubbling pool of sulfur. Calder reached for the radio-phone and beamed in the companion 'copter.

"Dr. Uhl! I think we've spotted the animal. It looks like it's after the sulfur pits. We're going in."

"Right," the Doctor said. "Only give us a chance to follow you,

Colonel. Don't forget—we're the boys with the net.

"I won't," Calder said tightly. His lips and eyes were grim.

They could see the creature raising its awesome head, now larger than before, at the sound of the approaching motors.

"Circle him!" Calder said.

"Look for a clear spot for us to land in."

The whirlybird dropped lower, heading straight for the creature. It spun about, its jaws snapping in hatred at the annoying sound of the spinning rotors.

"Here they come!"

They saw the second helicopter appearing to the left, its steel-wired net hanging beneath the fuselage. The creature saw it, too, and its head moved uncertainly, not sure which strange Earth-bird was going to attack first. It turned and headed for the shadows of a large rock.

"Damn!" Calder said. "We can't use the net unless we get it out in the open!"

"Maybe if we fired at it—"

"Wouldn't do any good. The thing's impervious to bullets . . .Wait! We'll drop some of the nice pure sulfur out of the 'copter. Maybe that'll tempt our friend!"

They guided the craft towards the cowering beast and Calder reached behind him for a sulfur sack. They opened the hatch, and he sent the sack plummeting towards the ground, not fifteen yards from the creature. Swiftly the 'copter rose again, just as the sack burst open and spilled the powdery stuff over the ground.

"Once more! Calder yelled.

Another sack went hurtling towards the creature, missing him by only a few feet.

"You ever been a bombardier, Colonel?" the pilot grinned.

"Look! It's working—"

The creature was emerging from its hiding place, its nostrils sniffing the good smell of the raw sulfur.

Calder grabbed the radio-phone. "It's taking the bait, Doc. We're ready to move now!"

"Okay. Stand by!"

The second helicopter was moving slowly to the scene. The creature, sorely tempted by the food it craved, was heading cautiously towards the spilled sulfur. Then its taloned hand was scooping it up, stuffing it between its dragon-like jaws, filling its ravenous stomach.

"Doc's ready to move in," Calder said tautly. "Put us down on the other side of those rocks."

The pilot nodded.

The moment they touched ground, the hatch opened and the armed men sprung out, their carbines ready.

"Bring that generator out here!" Calder said. "And for God's sake, keep out of sight of that thing!"

Swiftly, moving with as little noise as possible, the soldiers performed the unloading operations, ducking low behind the rocks to avoid the eyes of the creature.

"Here she comes." Calder's eyes were on the second 'copter. Let's have that walkie-talkie."

A soldier handed him the instrument. He put his mouth to the receiver and said: "Easy, Doc, easy. You're almost over the beast now. Just a little more . . . get as close as you can . . ."

Then—

"Drop it!

Overhead, they saw the second helicopter sway directly over the creature, and the steel-wired net fell free of the undercarriage. Despite its weight, it seemed to hand to long in the air—then it dropped heavily toward the creature.

They heard the beast's scream of rage as the weight of the net knocked it to the ground. It began struggling for freedom at once, its talons ripping at the steel threads its feet lashing out furiously.

"Now!" Calder said.

The armed soldiers ran towards the scene, with the Colonel leading the charge. Bringing up the rear came two men carrying the portable generator.

"Hold him down! Don't let him out!"

The soldiers hurried towards the edges of the net, and tried to prevent the beast from thrashing its way free. Quickly, they tried to drive the net into the ground with spikes, but the creature's wild movements made it impossible.

By now, the second 'copter had come to roost, and Calder was shouting: "Cable!"

One of the men with the generator came running towards the net, dragging an electric cable, an open clamp on the end. The other poised at the switch, waiting for the Colonel's signal.

"Clamp it! Now!"

The contact was made.

"Jump free!" the Colonel yelled. "Hit it!"

The man at the generator was staring blankly at the thing beneath the net. Dr. Uhl came racing to his side. He reached over and depressed the activating switch.

With a horrendous shriek and a violent upheaval of its body, the creature reacted to the electrical charge coursing through the steel wires of the imprisoning net.

Then, with a moan, it lay still.

"Careful," Calder said. "Wait—"

The creature thrashed once more and lay still.

"We've done it! Dr. Uhl said, running towards the Colonel. "We've got him Bob!"

Calder said: "Cut the switch." When it was done he walked slowly towards the vast, ungainly hulk of the unconscious beast. Thank God," he said softly. "Now we can find out. Now we can learn how . . ."

Over the rise, dusty figures appeared and surrounded the scene.

It's the Commissario," Dr. Uhl said.

The police chief walked towards them slowly. He paused at the Colonel's side and looked down mournfully at the monstrous prisoner under the net.

"I am sorry," he said stiffly.

"For what?"

"Sorry that we did not find it first, Colonel. I know it is important to you, to have this thing alive. But I wish I had found it and destroyed it. I really do."

"It's worth more alive Commissario. That may be hard for you to understand. But the creature is our ticket back into space."

"Perhaps," the Commisario said gravely. "But only the devil could create such a monster, Colonel. What good is a world where others of this kind breed?

"What good was this world," Calder said gratingly, "when the dinosaurs roamed Sicily? You're being superstitious, Commissario. I thought you were a sensible man."

"Very well," the Commissario said, and waved to his men with an air of defeat.

CHAPTER VIII

Probing the Unbelievable

THERE was excitement in the air of Rome. It was a city accustomed to excitement, since the days when Caesar's legions marched
down its streets. But this excitement had a quality of its own. It cir-
culated in odd patches throughout the city: in the bars and taverns
where the newsmen gathered, in the office of the constabularies,
in the museos where whispered rumors told of something strange
and marvelous which had come to Rome. And yet it seemed as if
even the citizens in the streets knew that this day was different, as
if some subconscious sense informed them that Rome had been
changed by some momentous event, had become the headquarters
of an occurrence such as the world had never witnessed before.

But the center of the excitement was an impressive stone building set among the monuments of the ancient and eternal city, a

building whose façade bore the seal of the great United States of America.

All day long, people had been coming and going through the doors of the American Embassy, avoiding the bullet-firing of reporters' questions, ducking in and out of limousines, maintaining an air of mysterious secrecy concerning the conversations that were taking place behind the stone walls.

There had been world-reknowned scientists spotted among the visitors, dignitaries from virtually every country in the free world, military figures resplendent in the uniforms of America and Italy.

In the Embassy anteroom a crowd of buzzing newsmen stood around impatiently, waiting for some official word. The majority were sober-faced, middle-aged men who wore the subdued, slightly fatigued look of the foreign correspondent, representatives of newspapers and news services that spanned the world. There were women among them, too, who if anything, were even more impatient than the men. Two Marines, sturdy and implacable in their full dress uniforms, flanked an inner door, looking impassable. The sound of speculating talk was everywhere.

"I don't get it," one journalist said. "Maybe they've rounded up some Soviet spies."

"I don't think so. I think it's another cabinet crisis—"

"Then why all the scientists? I'll bet its got something to do with nuclear tests—"

"You're crazy. Why is it in Rome?"

Round and round the conversations went, until the inner door suddenly opened and a bland faced attaché put his head outside.

All talk stopped.

"If you will come in please," the attaché said politely.

There was no hesitation in the forward movement of the crowd. They pushed eagerly towards the doors.

Once inside, they saw that chairs had been arranged for their convenience, facing a podium at the end of the room. There were two military figures flanking the podium. One was a bull-necked Major General; the other was a tense-faced young Colonel. Seated beside them was a white-haired dignitary representing the Italian Government; most of the local correspondents recognized him as Signore Contino. On a wooden table to the left of the podium, there was a bank of telephones.

"You will find seats please," the attaché told them. They separated quickly, vying for the best viewing position. The General, busily consulting a sheaf of papers in his lap, seemed oblivious to the excitement his presence had caused.

After a moment, when the room was silent he got up and went to the podium.

Good morning, ladies and gentlemen of the press.

He saw them flip open their notebooks.

"As you are all probably aware, there was an aircrash ten days ago off the coast of Sicily. There have been many rumors concerning that air tragedy. Not until now have I received permission from my government to give you the facts exactly as they are at this time."

The crowd stirred, and General McIntosh picked up a cablegram from the podium.

"This cablegram has been signed by the United States Secretary of Defense. It reads—'In the face of widespead speculation, and after consultation with various foreign governments, the President has authorized release of all information to press and news agencies for their immediate publication.'"

He looked up again. From his chair, Colonel Calder watched the General, and a faint smile came to his lips. He sensed that there was something of the showman in McIntosh's manner. The General knew he had a fascinated audience, and was making the most of the moment.

"I have prepared a statement," he continued, and flipped the papers in his hand.

"The airship XY-21 which crashed into the Mediterranean Sea on the eleventh, was a single-stage Astral propelled rocked launched thirteen months ago from a site within the United States. You will understand why I cannot mention the exact place.

The correspondents murmured in excitement at this announcement.

The rocket, with seventeen men landed on the planet Venus—"

Now the reaction seemed to explode among the General's audience, in audible cries of surprise and wonder.

"Venus!"

"The planet Venus!"

The General waited patiently until their voices subsided.

"This expedition has been in the making for almost four years. Its secret has been as well kept as the Manhattan Project of World War II. The planet Venus was chosen as our primary destination because of certain discoveries by the Palomar Observatory almost six years ago, discoveries that are now public knowledge. There are mineral elements on the planet that are considered of great value to the world; radioactive elements sufficient to supply the requirements of atom power plants for countless generations. This fact alone has made our expedition to Venus of vast economic and strategic importance. There are other considerations, too. Some of them might be regarded as—He paused, and looked at Colonel Calder with a smile. "You might say actually spiritual."

Calder hid his answering grin.

"The seventeen men chosen for this hazardous journey had to undergo what is probably the most rigorous training program known to modern history. The full details of that program, as well as other pertinent and non-classified facts concerning the expedition, will be covered in a report now in preparation in Washington."

"The expedition was successful. The landing was made on Venus, and special breathing apparatus employed to enable the crew to survive in the oxygen-less atmosphere of the planet. However, after a few days of exploration, the equipment mysteriously failed. An unidentified poison in the atmosphere attacked the crew. Eight died on the planet and were buried there. I will not reveal their names as yet. This will be done later."

The crowd hummed.

"The other crewmen managed to leave the planet before the strange poison took their lives. But misfortune still dogged their trail. On the return flight to Earth, the XY-21 was struck by a meteor, and the ship was irreparably damaged. It plunged into the sea off the fishing village of Gerra in Sicily. There was an heroic rescue of the one survivor of that crash—Colonel Robert Calder, seated beside me—the pilot of the XY-21 and Commander of the expedition."

Now the heads were turned to Calder's direction. The Colonel looked at the floor.

McIntosh placed his papers on the podium.

"Now I must bring you up to date, to tell you why we have come to Rome and called this press conference. There were specimens brought back from the planet Venus, specimens mineralogical, botanical and—animal. In the crash of the spaceship, all but one specimen was lost. That one, fortunately, was the most valuable, because it represented the embryo of a Venusian creature for which we have as yet no name."

Then the General's hand went up to command silence.

"Yes, that is the creature you have been hearing rumors about, the monster now confined in Rome's zoo. A beast from Venus, a strange an alien thing unlike anything evolution ever produced on our planet. But this animal represents more than a zoological curiosity. It may provide us the key to the secret of survival on Venus. We know now that the atmosphere is poisonous to humans, and that no second assault on the planet is possible until we devise equipment that will work effectively against this poison. And no such equipment can be devised until we understand the breathing mechanism of the monster now in the Rome zoo.

From the front row, a correspondent shot his hand into the air.

"May we be permitted to see the creature?"

"I'm going to ask you correspondents to select three of your number to accompany Colonel Calder to the zoo tomorrow morning. Those selected by you will, of course, pool the interviews with the entire press corps. We will supply you later with all the necessary photographs."

He looked about him.

"I guess that's all," he said, with a hint of humor on his mouth. "Thank you for your patience."

The newsmen needed no further signal. Excitedly, they scurried, jumped, and ran to the table with the telephones, or to the exit doors. Some of them tried to reach General McIntosh and the

Colonel, but the two WSAF officers headed swiftly for a side door, guarded by Marines.

"Some old friends," Mcintosh grinned as they came into the room.

Calder saw the scholarly face of Dr. Leonardo, wreathed in a gentle smile. Marisa's smile was less certain. She stuck out her hand formally and Calder took it.

Dr. Uhl arranged this permission for us," Dr. Leonardo said. "We merely wished to pay our respects."

Calder's eyes were on the girl.

"How are you, Marisa?"

"I'm all right. I—I heard about the capture of the creature from Dr. Uhl. It must have been frightful—"

"The worst is over," Calder said. "The beast is nice and tame now. We've taken all the fight out of him,"

"Colonel Calder." Dr. Leonardo touched his arm. "I have been assisting with the beast, as you know. But I am accustomed to having the help of my granddaughter. She is qualified, as you know—"

"I know," Calder grinned. "Almost-a-doctor. Sure, Dr. Leonardo, Marisa's help will be appreciated. Besides, it's really *your* creature when you come right down to it. Little Pepe sold it to you—for two hundred lira."

Marisa shivered, and Calder put his hand on her arm.

"It won't be pleasant. The thing has grown even more since we brought it down from the mountains. If you're afraid—"

"I'm *not* afraid!" the girl said stubbornly.

"Then you've got a job."

In the morning, the three correspondents chosen by the newsmen's vote met Colonel Calder in front of the American Embassy.

One of them was a tall correct Englishman named Maples, whose eyes held a skeptical gleam. One was an American newspaperman by the name of Briggs, who couldn't keep the grin off his face. The third was a business-like woman in a mannish gray suit named Hulda Reynolds, and it was she who kept firing questions at the Colonel as they waited to enter the Embassy limousine.

"I'm sorry," Calder said politely. "You'll just have to wait until we get there, Miss Reynolds. You'll know about our monster friend soon enough."

"This wouldn't be some kind of high-level gag, would it Colonel?" The American correspondent lit a cigarette. "I mean, what the heck, Bug-eyed monsters and stuff; that's funny-paper material."

"We didn't think it was so funny, Calder answered coldly. "Not when the thing almost killed a farmer up in Messina. Not when it tore out the throat of a dog. Not when we dropped a steel net over the beast, and had to knock it out with a jolt of electricity."

The answer silenced them, except for the Englishman. And all he said was "Astonishing . . ."

When the car finally arrived, Miss Reynolds climbed into the rear and said.

"But couldn't you tell us about your side of the story, Colonel? About what Venus was like?"

"That will be part of the final summation report from Washington. But I'll tell you this much. It's a world out of a madman's dream. Full of yellow dust clouds and desert and fog. You can't see more than a few feet ahead of you, and then all you see is misty and blurred. . ."

"What about gravity? Did you float?" Miss Reynolds giggled.

"No, there's hardly a difference. But you never see the sunlight or the stars. I got the feeling that it was newborn, smoldering . . ."

It wasn't a long drive to the Rome zoo, but the atmosphere was moody in the limousine by the time they reached it, the correspondents strangely effected by the Colonel's words. When they got out of the car, the American named Briggs recaptured his good humor, and grinned at the animals in their cages.

"Been a long time since I went to the zoo. Never heard a lion roar in Italian before."

The sound of trumpeting caught their ear.

"Or an elephant, either," Briggs said. "Hiya, Jumbo." He waved casually at the gray mammoth behind the huge cage. It lifted its trunk in salute.

"This way," Calder directed.

They went around the elephant cage to the site of a smaller cage guarded by two armed Roman policemen. Colonel Calder led them through the gate to a door cut in the side of an enormous cement structure. There was another officer there, and Calder spoke to him briefly. He saluted, and pushed the door open.

"What kind of place is this?" Miss Reynolds asked.

"It's the elephant house," Calder told her. "It was the only place we could keep the beast. I think you'll see why in a moment.

The sound of slow, labored moaning was constant in the large room they found themselves in. The correspondents didn't remark upon the sound, until they saw its source.

"Holy jumping—"

"Incredible!"

"A nightmare!"

They stood in stunned silence before the gigantic jerry-built wooden table about seven feet from the floor level, easily twenty-five feet long and twenty feet across. It was just about large enough to hold the monstrous beast that lay unconscious and moaning on its surface.

A strong metal band girded the creature's midriff and imprisoned him to the table, permitting the scientists and technicians in attendance to perform their mysterious and complex examinations of the creature's body. One attendant, standing on a raised platform with three steps, maneuvered a block and tackle connected to a shining steel chain around the creature's left wrist. He pulled on the device, and the three-taloned hand rose into the air. Its right hand was chained to the table.

They watched as the technician carried an electric wire, clamped by cathodes to the wrist of the beast, to a complicated control panel studded with illuminated dials and gauges. There were other such electrical boards around the room, winking and humming, incongruous in the elephant house of the Rome zoo. A small industrial Fork-Lift rolled across the stone floor.

Dr. Uhl was at one end of the table, supervising the activity of the attendants. Several white-coated scientists, their faces absorbed, were employing a variety of instruments to the scaly hide of the oblivious beast. Among them, Calder recognized Dr. Leonardo, aided by his granddaughter Marisa. Her motions were sure as the Doctor murmured his instructions, but there was an elusive light of horror and loathing in the girl's eyes.

It was Miss Reynolds who was first able to overcome her awe and speak.

"The—the size of the thing! It must weigh a ton!"

Calder spread his hands.

"And only eight days ago the creature was only this tall. We're not even certain that the growth process is over yet.

The Englishman tugged at a suddenly tight collar. "How do you account for such an astounding rate of growth, Colonel Calder? Or is that normal on Venus?"

"No, we don't thing so. Our scientists here believe that the Earth's atmosphere has upset its metabolic rate. The more it breathes, the more tissue it builds—and the bigger it gets. Now if you'll all come this way—"

They hesitated for a moment, and then followed Colonel Calder closer to the scene of the activity.

He directed them towards the rear of the great table, where the creature's fantastic tail hung limply. The electric cable clamped to its hide was attached to a panel that was being carefully observed by a bristly-haired man of mid years. His eyes didn't leave the spinning dials as the Colonel and the correspondents approached.

"You may have heard of Dr. Hans Albert of Vienna," Calder said. "He was flown here specially; probably the world's top expert in anesthesia."

Dr. Albert glanced up, smiled shyly, and his gaze returned to the dials.

"It's the Doctor's job to keep the creature unconscious during its examination. On Venus, we discovered that these animals are highly susceptible to electrical current. You will note the wire running to the creature's wrist. Dr. Albert keeps eighteen hundred volts of electricity coursing through its body. More voltage and it would die—less and it would awaken."

"Amazing," Miss Reynolds said, busily scrawling in her notebook.

"You can have a closer look at the wrist connection this way."

Calder led them up the small stairway to the platform, upon which the technicians maneuvered the heavy equipment necessary to move the beast into position for study.

There was a scientist directing the hoisting of the creature's right hand, and the correspondents noted his Oriental features with interest.

"Regular United Nations," Briggs muttered. "Our friend from Venus should be flattered."

Two workmen in clean smocks were passing a steel sling around a turbine, and attaching a huge iron hook. As the taloned right hand swung upwards, the newsmen looked in awe at the thickness of the dangling wrist.

"You will be careful, Please?" The Japanese scientist addressed the workmen courteously.

"This is Dr. Koroku of the University of Tokyo," Calder said quietly. "He is assisting Dr. Uhl, the civilian scientist in charge of the Venusian project.

"What's the turbine for?" the Englishman asked. "Another attempt to pry secrets from the creature?"

Dr. Koroku smiled. "We hope this electro-dynamometer will enable us to complete our examination of the aural passages."

Miss Reynolds poised her pencil. "Could you give us any statement on your progress so far.

The Japanese scientist looked at Calder, who nodded.

"So far," he said, "we have come to only one conclusion. The creature's olfactory system is more highly developed than any known on this planet."

Calder said: "We'll find Dr. Uhl on the other side of the platform. Maybe he'll have something further to tell."

The creature's labored breathing became louder as they moved timorously down towards the head of the beast. They saw Dr. Leonardo and his granddaughter, standing near by its frightening jaws.

"This is Dr. Leonardo, a prominent zoologist," Calder said. "It was Dr. Leonardo who first had possession of the egg from which the creature hatched. The girl beside him is his granddaughter, Marisa. She's—almost-a-doctor." He grinned to himself and Miss Reynolds looked at him sharply.

"What was that, Colonel?"

"Nothing. Let's get closer and see what they're doing/

They saw the girl hand the old man a beaker containing a clear blue liquid. He lifted the 100-cc veterinary syringe and hypodermic in his hand.

"Sixty-seven cc's" Marisa said. "Correct?"

"Exactly." He poured the contents of the beaker into the syringe.

"They're feeding the creature," Calder said in hushed tones. "It's a compound of sulfur. Sulfur serves the beast as our vitamins serve us."

Miss Reynolds' business-like air was vanishing as she realized their proximity to the very head of the creature on the table. But just as her face was showing feminine horror, Marisa's face was brightening as she spotted the approach of Colonel Calder.

"Will you need me any more, grandfather?"

"Eh? No, mi cara. Grazie."

She smoothed her hair and smock, and came towards the four spectators.

Calder smiled at her. "Hello Marisa."

"You caught me unprepared," she said, brushing a cloud of sulfur powder from her hands. "I've been cooking over a hot creature all day . . ."

"You look all right to me." He drew her aside, letting the correspondents move on alone. "As a matter of fact, you look better every time I see you. Or is it the light in this room?"

She twisted her mouth wryly. "Maybe it's the contrast. Next to *that* I look dandy. When you're free Colonel, I must tell you of my latest nightmare. . ."

Calder looked towards the newsmen, who were separating around the table, gazing in fascination at the chained creature, their hands busily scrawling notes.

"They're doing okay. Let's hear it now."

She looked at the floor. "It concerned a dark cafe—a small table—and a bottle of wine."

"And a burning candle?"

She nodded slowly, and her voice became ominous.

"The candle was burning lower, lower . . ."

"No!"

"Soon it will burn out!"

Calder looked at his watch and grinned. "If we hurry, maybe we can find that dark cafe before it starts getting too late."

Marisa smiled back, and began untying the strings of her smock. "We can try, Colonel. I'll go and change."

Calder turned to the correspondents as Marisa hurried off.

Now if you'll come with me, Dr. Uhl is expecting us."

Reluctantly, the correspondents left the platform and followed the Colonel towards the main control board where Dr. Uhl waited.

Calder introduced them, and Dr. Uhl said:

"Colonel Calder informs me that you wish to hear about our guest from outer space. It's hard to know where to begin."

Miss Reynolds prompted: "General McIntosh said it was important to learn how the animals survive the poisonous atmosphere of Venus." She looked at Calder. "If they find out, Colonel—does this mean you'll return?"

"Somebody will," Calder answered. "Somebody must."

"If you'll step over here," Dr. Uhl said, "I can show you what we're trying to achieve."

At a work table, he lifted a sheaf of reports.

"We found that the creature's respiratory system includes a sort of fibrous filtering element which blocks the poisonous vapors on the planet. Fortunately, we think we can duplicate that system almost exactly. With the help of this."

He picked up a spongy substance and handed it to Briggs.

"It's like a plastic sponge," the newsman said.

"It is made from one of the new synthetics," the Doctor told them. "With this filtering agent as the heart of our new breathing apparatus, we believe that Man can survive the next expedition to the planet. Still, a great deal of testing quite naturally remains to be done."

Maples, the Englishman said: "By the way, Doctor—there's a rumor that gunfire has no effect on the beast. Why is that?"

"Because the creature has no heart or lungs. Instead, it has a network of small tubes throughout its body. Hence small arms effect no damage. However, anything larger—canons, bazooka fire, that would finish him."

"Then he's hostile," Miss Reynolds said. "We'll have to fight him for his planet."

"No!" Calder said sharply. We encountered no hostility from the creatures on their home world. It was only when the beast was transplanted, tortured, staved—that's when the trouble started."

There was a sudden signal from the platform. They looked up to see Dr. Koroku gesturing at them.

"Please," he said loudly.

"You will please step backwards?"

They moved aside as the great iron hook swung the electro-dynamometer across the roof of the elephant house. The cable grated and clanked overhead, and—

"Look out!"

A terrified voice called up from below as the chain, with gathering momentum, swung the equipment off its course towards a network of dangling wires.

"The cables! Look out for the cables!"

The result came instantaneously, blindingly. The turbine-like equipment struck the lines and a flash of white light illuminated the room, defining sharply the startled features of the occupants. Sparks flew from the short-circuited wires in a fiery shower. At the electrical board controlling the anesthetizing voltage, Dr. Albert shouted in alarm as the illuminated panel abruptly went black.

"Short circuit! he said piercingly. "The board is out—"

The voltmeter swung down from 1800 to zero, and the board began to smoke.

All over the elephant house, the lights blinked out, leaving only the haze of daylight glowing through the skylight.

"The chains!" Calder yelled. "Watch that block and tackle!"

The stunned attendants guiding the pulley mechanism that held the beast's upraised right arm had ceased their activities as the lights went. Now they had lost control of their equipment, and the chain began to grind and slip.

"Look out for the hand—"

With a crash, the creature's hand landed in a maze of paraphernalia on the platform. The reverberation knocking one of the technicians off his feet. Debris fell everywhere, but all eyes were watching the creature.

It's coming around!" Dr. Uhl said.

"Not yet," Calder said crisply. "Everyone off that platform. Fast!"

The correspondents were the first to obey, heading for the exits. Dr. Albert was still at the board, trying to coax life back into the dead controls, hopelessly spinning dials. The Colonel vaulted towards him and pulled him away from the useless machine.

"It's no good, Doctor. The power's gone—"

"But the creature—"

"I said let's get out of here!"

Dazedly. Dr. Albert allowed the Colonel to direct him towards the exit of the building, while the other scientists and technicians made their way to safety.

Calder collared Dr. Uhl. "We've got to get the power back on. How long do you think it will take?"

"Hours," the Doctor shrugged. "We can't wait that long, Bob. We'd better get help—"

"Look!"

They turned to the creature again. Its head began a slight roll from side to side and a deeper groan escaped its jaws.

"Everybody back!" Dr. Uhl shouted.

Calder spotted Marisa dressed in street clothes, her eyes terrified. He waved at her in warning, just as the creature's tail began a slow gyration.

"We're in for it," Calder muttered. "If those clamps and chains don't hold—"

The creature struggled to sit up, and found itself bound. It strained furiously against the metal that held it prisoner. It roared in protest and increased its exertion until the metal began to crack.

"He's getting free!"

"Outside!" Calder commanded. "Everybody outside!" He pointed his arms towards the doorway. They heard the platform timbers begin to go as the creature thrashed in its struggle for freedom.

They were all out of the doorway by the time the last chain was thrown contemptuously aside from the creature's body, and it was raising itself defiantly to its full and terrifying height.

CHAPTER IX

Rampage!

Ray Harryhausen's rendering of the beast's rampage.

IN HIS office on the second floor of the American Embassy in Rome, a visitor was announced for Major General A.C. McIntosh. The General looked annoyed at the interruption, and then his face became grim when he heard the visitor's name.

"Senator Rufus Banyon," the secretary said. "He says the matter is urgent, General."

Senator Banyon, displaying all the bustle and authority of a committee of one, came into the room carrying a briefcase. He shook hands briefly and coldly with the General, and crossed his legs as he sat down.

"Is this an official visit?" the General said dryly. "Or just a Roman Holiday, Senator?"

The Senator laughed, showing fine white teeth.

"Perhaps a little bit of both, General. As you may know, our committee is concerned with foreign aid expenditures as well as— other matters. That entails a number of European visits. I made a special detour to discuss this subject with you."

"I'm honored."

"Thank you."

"Let's cut out the preliminaries," McIntosh said sourly. "It's my impression that your committee's authority over this project—if it ever had any—ended a long time ago, Senator. If you're here for a little sight-seeing, all right. But otherwise—"

"Your tone is a little arbitrary," Banyon aid, but with a smile on his face. "As a matter of fact, I don't think you're quite correct. Our authority may have ended as far as your *first* flight to Venus was concerned.

"What does that mean?"

The Senator fiddled with his briefcase. "I understand now that a *second* voyage is being contemplated. Nothing official, of course. But this study that is being made of the Venusian creature—its sole purpose is directed towards a second trip, isn't that so?"

"Perhaps. But it may also be academic research, Senator.

"Come now, General—"

McIntosh stood up angrily.

"Say your piece, Senator. You gave us a hard time on the first

They raised their weapons as the creature thundered its defiance.

voyage, but you were overruled. What makes you think you can win this time?"

Now the briefcase was open, and the Senator was shifting documents in his hand.

"Public opinion," he said curtly.

"What?"

"Public opinion, General McIntosh. Americans don't like waste, General—especially the waste of human life. We've been told that of the seventeen men that embarked on the XY-21, only one man has survived. That's a mighty low percentage, General. You'll have to admit that.

"I admit it."

"A greater percentage of men than any war might cost us, General. And yet this isn't war time, is it? This was definitely a mission of peace."

"Those men knew what risks they were taking. They knew what their chances of survival were. There's always sacrifice involved in any expedition involving human progress, Senator Banyon. Don't tell me that public opinion doesn't know *that.*"

Banyon sighed.

"Perhaps" he said. Perhaps they will become reconciled to this loss. But now we hear of another danger, General, besides the danger of meteor strikes and cosmic rays. We hear of a dreadful alien monster, something prehistoric and terrible—"

"Nonsense! The creature is an animal native to the planet Venus. It was brought back to Earth for a study of its breathing organs. It may appear to be a monster to us, Senator. But perhaps we look pretty terrible to it."

"Yet is *it* dangerous? Impervious to bullets? Gigantic in size—and perhaps still growing?"

"Not impervious to *all* arms, Senator. Not impervious to a simple electrical charge. Colonel Calder's crew had no trouble with the beasts on the planet. Their trouble was in the air itself, not the wild life. Man has conquered equally dreadful beasts. There's no danger there."

The Senator rubbed his jaw thoughtfully.

"I understand the creature has killed a man. A farmer wasn't it?"

"No. The creature killed only a dog, and maimed one man. But he still lives. And that was only because the old farmer provoked the creature into attack. He was frightened, foolish."

"Then in your opinion," Banyon said smoothly, "the creature is harmless?"

"Properly handled, yes. If this is going to be your argument against future space flights, Senator, you're going to have a hard time building a case. Not even this thing you call 'public opinion' will take you seriously, even if you play on their superstitious fears of dragons and such . . ."

Banyon closed his briefcase with a loud snap of the locks.

"Very well, General. I'm not here to bicker with you about this thing. You say the beast is harmless; I'll have to accept your opinion. But I still wouldn't count on having such an easy time putting your next little voyage together. There's also the matter of money, you know. We have some heavily-burdened taxpayers in the country."

"Good day, Senator," the General said.

"Yes, of course." Banyon smiled and got to his feet. "Good day, General." He walked towards the door, but turned before going out. "Where is the hideous creature now?"

"Strapped and unconscious and helpless," the General said. "In the Rome zoo, where our scientists are studying its body for its secrets."

"Then all is well?"

"All is well," McIntosh said grimly.

Calder slammed the door of the elephant house shut, the crowd of scientists and technicians milling behind him. In the cage to their right, the elephant lifted its trunk and trumpeted with uneasy excitement.

The Colonel looked about and spotted a uniformed zoo-keeper.

"You! he said curtly. "Get that elephant out of its cage and away from here!"

"But Signore—"

"You heard me!"

Within the elephant house came the sound of crashing equipment. The noises spurred the zoo-keeper into obedience. He headed for the cage of the frightened elephant and secured a long pole.

He prodded the mammoth towards the gate and down the path.

"The thing's trying to get out," Dr. Uhl said breathlessly, his eyes on the door of the elephant house. "He's grown stronger—I don't know if the cement will hold."

They heard the thudding of the creature's body against the door. Again and again, it hurled itself against the exit of its cement prison.

"It's beginning to buckle," Calder said, staring at the cracks appearing in the door.

They moved back as the cracks widened.

Then the creature burst through!

For a moment, the thing from Venus stood framed within the ragged opening his violent pounding had created in the cement of the elephant house. The elephant on the path, who was startled at the appearance of the thing, lifted its trunk nervously and bleated in fright. The keeper tried to control its movements with the pole, but the pachyderm raised its massive forefeet in the air.

The pole fell out of the keeper's hand. He reached down to retrieve it, just as the creature attacked.

Trumpeting first in fear, and then in responsive fury, the mammoth reared to meet the charge of the alien beast. The crowd broke and scattered, and then returned in a wide, awed circle to watch the struggle between the two gargantuan animals.

The creature, undismayed by the first counterattack of the elephant, sprung again with renewed savagery. It bulldozed its way towards the gray animal, ignoring its sharp tusks.

The keeper shouted, and tried to use his pole to get the elephant away from the conflict. A news photographer emboldened by the opportunity for a sensational picture, hurried closer with his camera poised.

With a roar, the creature tore at the throat of the elephant with its taloned hands, and the violence of its attack sent the gray mammoth off its feet.

"Look out!" the crowd shrieked. But it was too late to warn the two men close to the scene of the battle. The elephant's massive body thudded heavily to the ground, pinning the cameraman and the zoo-keeper beneath tons of flesh and bone.

Marisa screamed, and clutched at Calder's sleeve frantically. He brushed her off and shouted to the crowd.

"Clear the area! Everyone clear the area! He whirled towards Dr. Leonardo. He shouted, "Where's the nearest phone?"

"It is there, Colonel." He pointed towards the left, and Calder hurried off.

The elephant was back on its feet now, edging away from the snarling creature that had come from space to do it battle. The creature moved after it, and the two combatants headed away form the park and into the streets of Rome itself, their animal cries resounding through the quiet avenues.

The crowd, both fearful and fascinated, pushed its way back and forth, eager to see they fray, yet frightened to suffer the fate of the men who had crossed their furious path. Then, suddenly, the battling animals changed their course and backed into the throng. Shrieking, they ran in mad panic from the danger.

Now there were horrible gashes torn in the side of the elephant, blood pouring freely from the wounds inflicted by the creature's raking teeth and talons. Still the mammoth fought on, with some stirring of primeval courage in its body. It fought as its mastodon ancestors might have the savage Tyrannosaurus Rex of the Earth's dawn.

But the struggle was in vain. The creature's unearthly strength asserted itself, pushing the elephant backwards, rending its tough hide with every slash of its talons, depriving the mammoth of life giving blood.

Then, with a monstrous shriek, the creature closed in for the kill. It dove straight for the elephant's throat, its fangs sinking deeply into the leathery flesh.

General McIntosh's face paled as he listened to the excited voice quivering in the telephone diaphragm. Beside him, Signore Contino stood waiting patiently.

"Right away, Bob," the General said. "Right away. I'll get down there as soon as I've ordered out the troops. Stay with the beast and get reports to me if you can. And watch yourself!"

He hung up, and leaned on the desk.

"Loose and on the rampage! There was a short-circuit in the elephant house. The anesthetizing equipment died. If the beast isn't stopped, it'll kill hundreds—maybe thousands. Two men are dead already, maybe more. We'll need men, artillery, tanks—immediately!"

Contino reached for the telephone. "Immediately!" he said hoarsely.

McIntosh beat his fist into his palm and went to the door. He shouted for his aide, and the Major appeared quickly.

"That Senator Banyon. Is he still in the Embassy?"

"No, sir. I understand he was going to the zoo, to see the creature."

The General groaned. "All right, Major. I'll be leaving for the zoo myself—just as soon as Signore Contino makes some arrangements.

The Major hesitated. "Something gone wrong, sir?"

"Everything," McIntosh snapped.

In a last brave effort, the elephant tried to shake the jaws of the creature loose from its bleeding throat. But the more it struggled, the more deeply the fangs penetrated.

Then the elephant's spirit waned, and it crashed to the ground. Fatally wounded, it trumpeted a last note of defiance, shuddered, and lay still.

Calder watched the conclusion of the combat from a distance, his mouth twisting. He looked about him and spotted a deserted staff car, its driver having joined the fleeing crowd that was pouring into the streets of Rome.

He jumped behind the wheel. The motor had stalled but he coaxed it back into action. He drove the auto straight towards the dying elephant, as the creature lumbered off after the mob. He stopped before the prone body.

Dr. Leonardo and his granddaughter came to him on the run, with Dr. Uhl following.

"Colonel!" the old man said. "Did you reach General McIntosh?"

"Yes. He's going to get artillery into the city right away. Dr.

Uhl, try and get a taxi. Take Dr. Leonardo and Marisa back to the Embassy. And tell the General that I'm going to track the beast as long as I can."

"Right."

As they moved away, Calder started the motor again, banking the car sharply in the direction the creature had taken.

There was panic everywhere, men and women running purposelessly, wild-eyed, some not even aware of what terror they were fleeing.

At last, Calder saw the creature.

It was posing incongruously against a stolid old building, roaring at the dispersing throng of citizens. Its arm lashed out, and its taloned hand closed around a nearby street lamp. The lamp buckled and the glass showered into the gutter. Its enormous tail swished menacingly, and then its other hand reached down to grasp one of the running figures in the street.

"No!" Calder shouted, stricken at the sight. He wanted to look away, but his eyes were held unwillingly by the spectacle. The woman in the creature's grip let out an unholy cry, and then the scream was squelched in her throat as the creature's fingers tightened about her.

The beast dropped the broken body to the ground and roared out to the world again.

A thought exploded in Colonel Calder's mind, and he started into action before his mind could consider the dangers. He shoved his foot down hard on the car's accelerator, and whipped the wheel about, driving the staff car head-on towards the lumbering beast.

The creature saw the attack, but too late to avoid it. The car bludgeoned into the beast's body, sending it toppling against the stones of the building. Calder struggled with the controls, but the car had stalled. He drove out the door and ran for the protection of a nearby doorway.

Furiously, the creature tried to regain its footing. He charged at the automobile that was pinning him against the building, and tipped it over on its side with a growl of rage. Then it scanned the scene for further assailants, and moved on.

Calder watched its progress from the doorway. When the creature disappeared around a corner, he left his place of concealment and followed.

Just as he came to the corner, he heard the splashing of water, and realized that the beast had flung itself into the Tiber River that flowed through the city. He hurried to the wall and peered over, looking for signs of the escaping animal. He saw nothing but the smooth surface of the water.

"Now we've really lost him," he muttered.

He walked away rapidly until the sight of a phone booth on the street stopped him. He jerked open the door and grabbed for the receiver.

General McIntosh pushed his way through the crowd of shouting newsmen, but the sharp, familiar voice at his side caused him to halt.

"So it's you," he grunted. "I see you didn't stick around the zoo very long, Senator."

"No," Banyon said viciously. "I saw enough of your harmless beast, General. I saw it kill four people—two of them women."

"We're dispatching an Italian Army contingent there immediately. The thing is swimming around in the Tiber; we'll stop it there."

"With bullets, General?"

"With grenades, with bombs, with tanks—with anything!"

The Senator smiled suddenly, looking around at the crowd of excited correspondents.

"Should make quite a news story, General. It'll be on all the news services in another hour, make interesting reading back home. What do you thin of 'public opinion' now, General?"

"It couldn't be helped—"

"No, no of course not. But I wouldn't say this improves your chances does it? For a second expedition?"

"You're wrong," McIntosh said coldly. "I think it'll take more than a rampaging monster to stop us, Senator. You can try all you like, But you'll lose."

"We'll wait," Banyon said. "We'll wait and see."

"Excuse me." The General shoved past him, on his way to the door.

The boulevard that faced the peaceful banks of the Tiber looked like a battlefield. Troops were deployed all along the edge of the river wall, and in the distance, the sound of exploding grenades punctuated the air. General McIntosh's staff car screeched to a halt, and Colonel Calder came running to the window.

"What do you think, Bob?" The General's voice was unsteady. "Will the hand grenades force the creature out of the water?"

"I don't know. I can't tell what the thing will do or when it will do it. All I know now is that they're blasting the Tiber straight through the city."

Signore Contino, his gray face showing the strain of the past hours, joined them.

"We are deploying tanks and artillery about the city," he said. "We are protecting our citizens in every way we can."

"How about casualties?"

"Twelve we know about."

Calder replied tightly. "Eight men and four women. But we're ready for the east now. As soon as it tries to leave the water—"

The staccato of exploding grenades increased.

Emilio Ferrara, a big sandy-haired soldier with a happy face, laughed suddenly. His companion, Guido looked at him as if the big fellow had gone mad.

"What's so funny?"

Emilio looked over the side of the bridge of Ponte St. Angelo and grinned.

"This bombing of the water. I feel like a schoolboy again, throwing rocks into the lake. What good do they think this can do?"

"I do not know," Guido grumbled. He reached out another hand grenade. He pulled out the pin and looped the weapon into the water. Both men ducked behind the bridge wall as the grenade exploded, sending a white spray over their heads.

"It's like a game," Emilio chuckled. "They say there is some kind of demon swimming in the river. A thing from the sky. It seems like a waste of good powder."

"Throw your grenade," Guido said sourly. "Leave the orders to the commander. If they wish us to bomb the Tiber, we bomb it. That is the Army."

"So be it," Emilio shrugged. He took a grenade from his belt, yanked out the pin with his teeth, and then threw it casually into the water."Here, my monster friend. A little plum to chew on."

He ducked just in time to avoid a burst of water in his face. Then he stood up and looked over the edge.

"Mother of God!"

"What is it, Emilio?"

Guido stood up and came beside him.

Out of the river, the water shining on its scaly hide, rose something out of a childish nightmare, a demon from the seas of medieval history.

"The beast!" Guido said. "Run, Emilio—"

But the sandy-haired man was fascinated. He yanked at his belt and produced his service pistol. He fired five shots into the ugly head without effect. Then the beast, with a roar, ducked beneath the bridge and disappeared.

"Come, Emilio!" his friend shouted. "We must tell the others."

"He is beneath us," Emilio said. "Quick—more grenades!"

They reached for the weapons and ran to the other side of the bridge. But the creature was no longer to be seen, Another soldier, carrying a walkie-talkie, came running in their direction. They shouted at him.

"The monster! We have found the monster!"

"Where?"

"Beneath the bridge," Emilio said excitedly. "I fired upon him, but he did not die. He is a devil!"

Just as the soldier put the walkie-talkie to his mouth, they heard the cracking sound beneath their feet. They stared in disbelief as the very concrete of the bridge split and widened and snapped, the ground rising into the air. The three men were toppled off their feet, and the head of the creature from outer space appeared over the wall.

Wildly, they fired their guns into the gleaming eyes as the center section of the bridge broke apart. The man with the walkie-talkie shouted desperately into the mouth-piece.

"Ponte St. Angelo, calling H.Q.! Ponte St. Angelo, calling H.Q.!

Again the monster's great bulk heaved against the concrete, and two of the Italian infantrymen were flung into the water.

In an Army car racing to the scene, Colonel Calder, the General, and Signore Contino listened grimly to the frantic message crackling from the car radio.

"Destruction—" the voice was saying. "Indescribable destruction at Ponte. St. Angelo—"

"Faster!" Calder told the driver, who shrugged his shoulders and pushed harder on the accelerator.

"Banyon," the General muttered.

"What's that?"

"Nothing. But every time a man dies at the hands of that creature, I keep thinking of Banyon's face."

"Why think of him? Calder said. "The Senator's rocking on his front porch. He can't bother us now."

"Maybe he can, Bob. He's here—here in Rome now."

"What?"

"He says he was in Europe on other business, but I don't believe him. I think he's readying his case now against the second Venus expedition. He's out to stop the flight before it begins. The monster's going to be his biggest argument. That's why we *must* stop the beast—fast!"

"This is it," Signore Contino said.

The car stopped, and they looked out of the windshield with pained eyes.

"Terrible," Contino whispered, looking at the demolished bridge and the row of dead bodies.

They scrambled out of the vehicle, and Calder headed for the squad of soldiers at the entrance to the bridge. One of them handed him a walk-talkie, and said:

"There is still one alive on the bridge. The man who broadcast to us. You can speak to him."

Calder grabbed for the instrument.

"Hello! This is Colonel Calder, U.S. Where is the creature now?"

The voice croaked back. "It has left the water. It is heading towards the Colosseum area. The beast is heading for the—"

"All right," Calder snapped. "Stay where you are and we'll get help to you."

He handed back the walkie-talkie and spoke to General McIntosh.

Deploy all forces to the Colosseum area. The beast is on his way.

CHAPTER X

Of Death and Love

Pepe, stiff and awkward in the new suit which Verrico had insisted upon him purchasing, as befitting to a boy of such great wealth, stood in front of the village general store.

He twisted a forelock of his dark hair and looked up at the row of cowboy hats from Taixas that hung on wooden pegs outside. He looked thoughtful, deliberating.

"Well, my little friend!"

Pietro, the shopkeeper, beamed at him from the doorway, twisting his moustaches in anticipation. The tale of Pepe's fortune had changed the boy's status in Pietro's eyes.

"And what can I do for the great Pepe today? Another cowboy hat from Taixas, perhaps. A good cowboy cannot have to many hats!"

"No," Pepe said.

"Ah, but then you must have the fine cowboy *suit* from Taixas. Straight from Roma! The wooly pants and spurs for the horse. The big shiny guns, with the real imitation leather holsters!"

"No," Pepe said.

"No?"

"No," said pepe stubbornly.

Pietro clucked. "And what happened to the great cowboy from Taixas? Are you not buying the big white horse to ride the great plains?"

"No, Signore Pietro. I would like instead the big spaceman hat. The fine space suit. You have these things?"

Pietro's face fell. "No little one. I do not carry such foolishness! So you no longer wish to be a great cowboy?"

Pepe sneered.

Cowboy games, they are for children! I am going to be a spaceman, and I shall travel to the moon. To the planet Mars! To Venus!"

Pietro scratched his head and Pepe looked upwards as the first star of evening twinkled in the Sicilian sky.

Then he walked away, his narrow shoulders thrown back in pride.

Verrico walked along the beach in the approaching twilight, his face mournful, carrying the cloth thing in his hand. Mondello came lumbering towards his companion on his short, stubby legs.

"What is that you have?"

Verrico lifted it in his hand. "It is a jacket I found in the cave by the beach, where little Pepe hid the American cylinder. It is from the great aircraft that sank in the sea."

Mondello looked at it.

"USAF," he said, reading the letters stenciled across the back. "What does this mean?"

"It is the name of the American flyer, that sent the big ship into the sky. It is the jacket of one of the men who went down to his death."

"It is sad," Mondello said, shaking his head. "These men, they must have been very brave to have done such a thing."

"Si," Verrico replied, looking at the jacket. "Tell me, Mondello, are your arms tired from hauling on the nets? Or is there strength yet in your body."

Mondello threw out his chest.

"I am as strong as ever!"

"Then come with me, Ondello, and we will speak to Father Antonio. We will ask his permission to dig a resting place behind the church for this flying jacket. We will dedicate the grave to all the good men who died in our waters."

Mondello hesitated at the thought of graveyards. But then he said:

"Si, Verrico. And it is *I* who will dig the grave. You look tired."

At the American Embassy in Rome, Dr. Leonardo patted his granddaughter's hand and said:

"You must not be upset, Marisa. Soon, they will find the beast and destroy it."

"It isn't that, grandfather."

She turned her lovely sea-green eyes aside.

"Oh? Then what troubles lie heavy on your pretty head? Soon you will be returning to America to complete your education, to be a fine doctor of medicine as you have always dreamed. Soon you will be able to forget all of this nightmare . . ."

Still his granddaughter looked unhappy, and the old man shook his head in understanding.

"Ah, I know what you are thinking. You are thinking of the Colonel Calder. Am I right, Marisa?"

She nodded somberly. "You are fond of Colonel Calder. And you wonder, perhaps, if he—" He put his arm around her shoulders. "I have lived a long time, mi cara. I have seen in the Colonel's eyes when he looks at you tells me but one thing. He, too, is fond

The mightiest beasts of two planets meet in combat.

of you, Marisa."

She looked up at him.

"But can a man have two loves, grandfather?"

"What do you mean?"

"This space voyage, this traveling to the planets and the stars . . . this is his real love, grandfather. There isn't room in his life for anything else.

"NO, you're wrong, Marisa. A man *can* have two loves. Sometimes, a man *must* have two loves to be happy—his life's work, and his life's mate. I love this foolish science of mine, Marisa, this study of the birds and animals that God has placed on our world. And yet I loved you grandmother, too, mi cara. In heaven she waits for me, and our love will bloom again, the way spring returns to the earth.

He stroked her hair gently.

"Do you understand, Marisa?"

Her eyes were shining when she looked up again.

"Oh, yes, grandfather. I do!"

The door of the office opened, and a brisk young Italian Major put his head in the doorway. When he saw the room's occupants, he nodded briefly and started out again, but Dr. Leonardo called to him.

"Major! Is there any word of the creature?"

"Yes, Doctore. They are closing in upon the animal now. It has left the Tiber."

"Where is it?" Marisa said, jumping to her feet.

"Yes," Dr. Leonardo said, with an amused smile.

"Where is *he?*"

The Major looked confused by what they were saying, but then replied:

"It is heading for the Colosseum."

The ancient Romans, who had erected the Temple of Saturn in tribute to their Gods, never knew what unworldly blasphemy would invade its graceful columns. Time has done enough damage to the structure, and it seemed as if the creature from an alien world had come to complete the task.

In the rubble surrounding the great ruins, Italian infantrymen moved in swiftly with ready carbines, trying for a shot at the creature's brain as it moved behind the columns. From the street, a tank appeared carrying a flame-thrower on its surface.

A boyish Lieutenant, his face eager and excited by his first combat mission, directed the movements of the men. When he spied the creature in the ruins of the Temple, he motioned wildly for the tank to move up.

"Fire when you see him!" he cried.

The snout of the flame thrower turned. The creature looked its way, as if recalling the episode on the mountaintop, and roared out in warning.

"Fire now!"

The flames spat forth, blackening the columns of the Temple, and making the beast cry out in agony and rage. Its huge tail lashed out and thundered against the weak stone monument; its great body pulled its way to the other end of the editice. Columns crumpled under its attack and more rubble crashed into the street.

"Look out!" the Lieutenant cried, as the old stones tumbled towards them, showering the infantrymen, raining crushing death at the heads.

With a final roar, the creature left the Temple of Saturn, and lumbered off to seek a more solid hiding place.

In the staff car, Colonel Calder looked at the General sharply as the voice on the car radio broadcast staccato reports of the beast's movements.

"The Colosseum," he whispered. If we can get it trapped in there—"

"Trapped," the General repeated wryly. "We've had the damn thing trapped a dozen times."

They drove through the streets until the vast bowl of the ancient Roman amphitheatre came into view.

"There it is!"

They had arrived just in time to see the creature from Venus, its back to the concrete walls of the stadium, hiss and growl at its tormentors. Then it turned its back to them and attempted to scale the structure in an effort to escape.

"He's getting away again," McIntosh said. "The thing's got a charmed life—"

"Maybe his luck's run out," Calder said. "Let's go."

They climbed out of the car, and an Italian Captain, whose beribboned uniform told of many campaigns, came to greet them. He saluted wearily, and said:

"It has climbed inside the Colosseum, General. My men could not prevent it."

"Just as well," McIntosh said. "If he's in there, we'll see that he doesn't get away. Let's get troops and tanks deployed completely around the stadium, not more than a few yards apart. We don't want any mistakes this time. And Captain—"

"Yes General?"

"With you permission, I'd like Colonel Calder here to take charge of your troops. He's had a lot of experience with the creature; I think he'll be useful."

The Captain looked relieved, "Gladly, sir." He walked beside the Colonel, talking eagerly. "I have fought many battles, Colonel, but never against an enemy like this. I fought with the American Army at Salerno. I was wounded twice, Colonel, and decorated by General—"

"Later," Calder said. "We'll talk about it later, Captain. Let's get those men with the bazookas inside. Get them in positions all around the arena. Remember—tell them to scatter!"

"Yes, sir!"

Calder looked up anxiously at the sky. The daylight was almost gone, and he knew that night was on the side of the creature.

When the Captain had gathered his forces, Colonel Calder headed for an entrance of the great monument to the ancient Roman way of life.

He couldn't help the awed look as he gazed around the vast ellipsoid that had once been the playground of the Emperors of the mightiest empire in all history. He looked at the eats that had once held some forty to fifty thousand shouting, gesticulating Roman citizens, out for a day of bloodthirsty sport and games . . .

Now there was a new kind of sport on the field of the Colosseum. But where was it?

A roar came from the north side of the arena.

Calder turned swiftly in the direction of the sound. From the seats, at the high vantage point some fifty yards from the Colonel a bazooka launched a missile in the same direction. Masonry exploded, and the creature roared out again in frustrated madness.

"Let's go!" Calder cried.

From all parts of the stands, the soldiers began moving cautiously forward, heading for the site where the creature had been fired upon.

"Watch out!" someone shouted as the thing came into view. It hissed and growled and seemed larger than ever.

"Keep moving in," Calder said. "He's got no place to go . . . keep moving forward."

But the beast was defiant still. With an ugly spreading of its jaws, it reached its taloned hands down and picked up a huge boulder of masonry. It lifted the object high over its head, and then hurled the massive bit of debris at the oncoming soldiers. One was knocked flat by the impact, his bazooka flying from his hand. Quickly, Calder leaped to grab the fallen weapon.

Now they were marching forward inexorably, and the beast, with its back to the high wall, roared at them all the louder, its claws raking the air, like some fearsome gladiator.

Calder lifted the bazooka to his shoulder. He took his time about sighting, and then fired.

The shot struck the creature's shoulder, and it spun about, screaming. Then it moved backwards again, until its scaly hide was against the Colosseum wall.

"Hurry!" the Colonel urged, racing after it.

But the creature was displaying a skill and tenacity that they never knew it possessed. Despite the time-worn smoothness of the concrete, despite the height of the wall, it put out its claws and gripped the old stones. It clung desperately, and began to move upwards. Before another bazooka missile could be launched, it had scaled the wall and was hoisting itself over.

But this time, the escape route wasn't clear.

Outside the amphitheatre, a ring of weapons were awaiting the beast from Venus, ready to fire.

"There it is!" McIntosh cried, as the ugly dragon's head appeared over the rim of the arena.

Signore Contino waved his arm frantically at the tank commander behind him.

The tank turret began to revolve, aiming towards the awesome head. The shell exploded out of its mouth, heading dead-aim for the creature on the Colosseum wall.

The creature was hit.

It staggered backwards, scraped its talons on the stone to hold its position, and managed to prevent a fall.

Inside the arena, Colonel Calder raised his bazooka once more.

The shot caught the creature squarely. It screamed in anguish and in dreadful realization, just as the tank outside fired its second shell. The ancient wall of the Colosseum crumpled under the bombardment, and debris and creature tumbled into the arena.

Calder looked at the dead beast and the rigidity of his features suddenly disappeared. His mouth drooped in weariness and relief, and his shoulders slumped.

Then he turned and walked to the entrance, not looking back.

His friends were waiting for him. The General, Signore Contino, Dr. Leonardo, Marisa. But Calder walked on without seeing them, away from the scene of death.

Dr. Uhl looked after him, not saying anything. Then he followed the others into the arena, to gaze at the dead creature lying in the rubble of ancient stone.

He looked at the beast and his voice was sad.

"Why is it always—*always* so costly—for man to move from the present to the future?"

No one answered him.

Marisa turned her eyes away from the sight, and scanned the departing crowd.

Then she broke into a run. She caught up with the Colonel and slowed her pace, walking silently beside him. He stopped to look at her, and his arm went around her waist. They walked back to the staff car together.

The cafe was dark, but the candle on the table shed a gentle light on Marisa's face revealing her look of contentment.

Colonel Calder hitched his chair closer to the table and put one of her hands in his. He held it wordlessly for a moment and then said:

"It took a long time to get here, Marisa. But does this fit all the specifications? I certainly hope so."

She looked around archly.

"Perfectly. Only one more thing required, Colonel. The wine.

"Naturally."

He beckoned to the waiter, and the short, grinning man with the clean white apron came over. But juts as he lifted out his order pad, the cafe manager was hurrying to their table.

"Please, signore, excuse me," he said nervously. "You are perhaps Colonel Calder, of the American Air Force?"

"Yes, that's me." Calder looked at him in puzzlement.

"What's up?"

"Beg your pardon, Signora," He looked apologetically at Marisa. "But a telephone call, a few minutes ago, from the American Embassy—"

"I knew I shouldn't have told 'em where I was," Calder said bitterly.

The manager shrugged. "I was informed that if a Colonel Calder came in, I was to give him immediately this message from the General Mac—" He gave up on the name and shrugged again. It is urgent, Signore."

Calder grimaced and scraped his chair back.

"This is one date that really gets postponed," he said. "I wonder what's up?"

"Maybe they found another egg—"

"Don't say such things. Listen, maybe the General won't need me for too long. Why not wait here a while? If I'm going to be detained more than half an hour, I'll ring here and let you know. All right?"

"Fine," Marisa said cheerfully. Then she bent over and blew out the candle. "We might as well save this .. ."

It was a short walk to the American Embassy from the cafe, and Colonel Calder covered the distance in less than five minutes. The surrounding street was dark, but lights were burning brightly on the second floor of the Embassy building.

Calder knocked on the door of the office assigned to General

McIntosh.

"Come in!"

McIntosh was at the window when Calder entered. He said: "Sorry to spoil your fun, Bob. But I thought you'd want to hear this news just as quickly as it arrived."

"What news, sir?"

McIntosh walked over to the desk and picked up a long white envelope, its wax seal freshly broken.

"This arrived by special courier from Washington about two hours ago. It's signed by the Secretary of Defense, and its contents are naturally classified. Frankly, I don't know if I'm doing the right thing by telling you about it. But I will tell you—because you're the one man in this world who really deserves to know."

"What is it, General?"

"It's official notification. It says we're beginning arrangements for the second Venusian expedition. The work starts immediately. The new breathing equipment has been ordered for manufacture. The new XY-22 will be built within the next eighteen months. The

appropriation has been voted, and Senator Banyon or anyone else will have to overrule the White House itself to get it changed.

The Colonel just stared at him.

"And pending another round of examinations," McIntosh said, "to make certain that these past months haven't affected our candidate's health, the pilot and commander of the next expedition has already been named.

The General put out his hand.

Colonel Calder shook it.

"Well," Marisa said. "That didn't take you long."

"No," Calder said. Please—let me do this." He lit the candle on the table.

They sat talking by its soft glow for almost two hours, until the flame was gutted by melting wax. Before it finally flickered out, Colonel Calder said:

"Will you marry me, Marisa?"

"What? Marry a man who'll disappear for months into the void? Who'll never be sure that he can come home? Who'll spend half his years in a spaceship or some terrible alien planet? Who loves space better than his own life? Yes," Marisa said.

THE END